Meet J.D.!

"What we mean to say," I tried to explain, "is that your grandma hired us to help out with the monkey."

"Big freaking deal," said Miss Joy Monroe. "Like I'm supposed to give a rat's—"

I cleared my throat real loud. "This is my little sister here, miss. She's not but seven, for your information."

"Oh, yeah?" The wolf girl made her green eyes go squinty. "And what's your name, little sister?"

Mary Al stood up real straight. "Mary Al," she said, sticking out her chin. "That stands for Mary Alice."

Miss Joy smiled an evil smile. Ain't no other way to describe it. I read about 'em in books, but I never had seen one live. "Well, my name's J.D." She batted her stubby eyelashes. "That stands for Juvenile Delinquent."

"By turns comic and heartrending, the story is propelled along by Jim's distinctive East Texan narration and populated by a cast of memorable characters."

—*The Horn Book*

"Nelson's insights about preadolescent grief are subtle and on the mark." —*School Library Journal*

"Recounts a memorable East Texas summer with immediacy and humor." —*Publishers Weekly*

"Energetically drawn from top to bottom." —*Booklist*

"You'll laugh, you'll cry and you'll love *The Empress of Elsewhere!*"
—Liz Moglia (The Mighty Liz), *New York Kids* (WNYC)

OTHER PUFFIN BOOKS YOU MAY ENJOY

the empress of elsewhere

a novel by

Theresa Nelson

PUFFIN BOOKS

PUFFIN BOOKS
Published by the Penguin Group
Penguin Putnam Books for Young Readers,
345 Hudson Street, New York, New York 10014, U.S.A.
Penguin Books Ltd, 27 Wrights Lane, London W8 5TZ, England
Penguin Books Australia Ltd, Ringwood, Victoria, Australia
Penguin Books Canada Ltd, 10 Alcorn Avenue, Toronto, Ontario, Canada M4V 3B2
Penguin Books (N.Z.) Ltd, 182-190 Wairau Road, Auckland 10, New Zealand

Penguin Books Ltd, Registered Offices: Harmondsworth, Middlesex, England

First published in the United States of America by DK Publishing, Inc., 1998
Published by Puffin Books,
a division of Penguin Putnam Books for Young Readers, 2000

3 5 7 9 10 8 6 4 2

The short story referred to on pages 157 to 159 is "A Sound of Thunder," from
The Golden Apples of the Sun and Other Stories by Ray Bradbury,
published by Avon Books.

LIBRARY OF CONGRESS CATALOGING-IN-PUBLICATION DATA
Nelson, Theresa.
The Empress of Elsewhere / Theresa Nelson.
p.   cm.
Summary: When he and his younger sister agree to help their wealthy, elderly neighbor
care for the capuchin monkey that keeps getting away from her, Jimmy also helps the
woman's troublesome granddaughter deal with secrets from her family's past.
[1. Friendship—Fiction. 2. Parent and child—Fiction. 3. Family life—Fiction.
4. Brothers and sisters—Fiction. 5. Monkeys—Fiction.] I. Title.
PZ7.N4377 Em 2000 [Fic]—dc21 99-054322
ISBN 0-14-130813-3

Printed in the United States of America

For my brothers and sisters,
Nelsons every one—

David Rogers,

Frances Katherine,

Thomas Harbert Hunter,

Mary Patricia,

Alice Carroll,

Annie Edmonston,

Jane Cullen,

James Keith,

John Henry,

and William Joseph,

with love from Theresa Anne

and—because we're the luckiest
eleven in the whole wide world—
for our parents, David and Carroll Nelson
of Beaumont, Texas

contents

I

GHOST | LIGHTS

First time I ever laid eyes on the Empress, she was skittering out the south gate of the Monroe mansion with her crown on crooked and her tail in the air.

I can see it all just as clear as Kodak, whether I want to or not. Reason I'm stuck with it? Second-worst day of my life.

I was out in the side yard when the whole mess started, trying to get old Ranger buried before the stink set in. My nose was running, my best friend had just moved to Phoenix, Arizona, and my dog was dead as a hammer.

And it wasn't even noon yet.

"Jim Junior! Mary Al!" Mama had just finished hollering out the kitchen window. "Y'all come on in here soon's you're done with that old dog, and I'll pour you some lemonade. That sun's gonna lay you flat."

"Yes, ma'am," I muttered. I shoveled another clod of rock-hard dirt and threw it on the grave. Poor old Ranger. Must have been the heat that got him, all right. East Texas sun could take out an elephant on a day like that, right slap in the middle of June. Never mind one bony, broken-down bird dog.

It was Mary Al found him. She'd run outside to watch the show next door, where Danny Brophy and his family were pulling out of their driveway in a crammed-up U-Haul, honking and hollering and waving good-bye. I was under my covers at the time, stopping my ears with both hands. But I could hear, all right. Not five minutes later she was back again, bawling her lungs out. "Ranger's dead," she blubbered, rooting under the bedspread and pulling on my arm. "There's goo in his eyes and ants crawling out."

"No, there ain't," I said, and I shook her off. I hated her telling such a fib. But Ranger was there, all right, dragged up stiff and staring in that pea-sized patch of shade under the Chinese tallow tree. Flies already circling.

Mama said I best bury him quick before the neighbors started complaining. I was pretty mad and almost said maybe Ranger wouldn't have died if she'd let him inside where he could be cool like everybody else's dog, but then my throat closed up on me so I never said a word. Which is probably just as well, now that I come to think of it. Mama don't brook that kind of sass.

Anyhow, there I was, sweating like a mule and throwing down dirt clods on the best dog ever was or will be, and there was Mary Al standing there watching me with her nose running, too, and her eyes all watery and red. Well, shoot, she wasn't but seven.

Right then pure hell broke loose.

It happened so fast, I didn't have time to be surprised. One minute I'm bending over Ranger's grave with a shovel full of clay; the next I'm knocked flat on my face by a pack of wild-eyed girls, screaming and hollering and chasing after some crazy little blur of goldy brown fur and silver spangles that's darting out through the traffic on Gilbert Street.

Cars honked. Brakes squealed. Drivers shook their fists.

"Hey!" I yelled, spitting out dirt balls and picking myself up. "What do y'all think you're doing?"

"Get it! Get it! Don't let it get away!" the banshee women wailed all together, pointing and screeching and pulling me after them.

"Get what? What is it, one of them little yippy dogs?" I never thought much of that ratty-looking breed, myself, but I figured I ought to go along and see could I help. Looked like these girls had the poor puny pup scared half to death, got it dressed up in doll clothes or some such fool thing. No wonder it was running.

"Ain't a dog!" a skinny girl panted, just as the whatever-it-was went leaping over the cyclone fence between our place and the park next door. I followed and made a grab, but my fingers closed on air, and before I was close enough to get another look, the critter had clambered up the nearest live oak and disappeared in a mess of trembly green leaves.

"So what is it, a squirrel?" I asked, best I could over all the shrieking. "Shoot, you can't keep a squirrel for a pet. Y'all ought to just leave it a—*ow!*" I yelled, as a hard green acorn with one of them little pointy tips hit me smack between the eyes. "What kind of a squirrel *is* that?"

"It's not a squirrel; it's a monkey!" sobbed another girl—a short kid with big shoes and fat red hair who looked like she was about to pass out. "It belongs to Old Lady Monroe's brat granddaughter, and she'll *kill* us when she finds out—"

"Finds out what?" I asked, dodging another green bullet.

"That we let her stupid monkey go—*ow!*" said the skinny girl. "*Ow!* Stupid—*ow!*"

"Quit whining, Francine, it was you let it go. Don't try to blame it on us!"

"Well, it was your idea about the dress."

"Was not!"

"Was too!"

"Hold on a minute!" I shouted. *"Would somebody please tell me what's going on?"*

The skinny girl—Francine?—rolled her eyes. "We already *told* you. We were over at Miz Monroe's to meet her grandkid, and—"

"Over *where?*" I interrupted, not believing my ears.

"Over *there*," said Francine. She pointed across the street to the Monroe mansion, the biggest, oldest, richest place in town.

Mary Al about fainted. *"Mrs. Million Dillion's?"*

It was an old family joke, was all, but I felt my face firing up. "No way," I said, quick as I could, before anybody had a chance to giggle. "Nobody goes over there."

Francine just shrugged. "Well, we did. Our mothers made us. But that's the last time! The kid's a real pill, and she has this stupid monkey—"

"And she *bit* me!" the fat-haired girl sniffled.

"The monkey bit you?" I asked.

"No, the *kid* did," said the girl, and then everybody started talking at once.

"So Miz Monroe locked her in her room—"

"The monkey?"

"No, the *kid*—"

"You shoulda heard her cussing."

"The old lady?"

"No, the *kid*!"

"But then she got loose—"

"The kid?"

"No, the *monkey*."

"And we'll never catch her now. *Ow! Ow!*"

The acorn missiles were raining all around us again, while the four girls screeched and ran eight ways at once.

"Just forget it!" Francine yelled. "That monkey's too mean to mess with. I'm calling my mama to take me home!"

"Me, too!" cried two of the others.

"Wait for me!" sobbed the fat-haired girl.

And with that they went tearing off across the park toward the pay phones at Chubby's Fried Chicken.

CHAPTER two

"Now what?" said Mary Al, when the dust had settled.

"Now nothing," I said. "We go home, that's all. Call the pound or the SPCA, one."

Mary Al cocked her head at me and scratched a chigger bite. "Ain't they the ones put strays to sleep?"

"Not if they know who they belong to. Not if they're tame."

Oak leaves rattled like a threat. Two more acorns hit the dirt—*Blim! Blim!*

"What if they ain't tame?" asked Mary Al.

"Shoot, I don't know. Come on, Mary Al. Ain't any of our business, anyhow."

I turned to go, but when I checked back over my shoulder, Mary Al was still standing there, talking baby talk into the branches. "Hey, little monkey. Come on down here, now. We won't hurt you."

"Get away from there, Mary Al. That monkey's liable to put your eye out with one of them nuts."

"No, she won't. She ain't mean, Jim Junior! Look there—see how she's watching us? She's just scared, is all."

Well, you might just as easy argue with a tree stump as with Mary Al, so I went ahead and looked where she was pointing, and sure enough I could see the monkey pretty clear now, hunkered down on a good-sized bough. Looking more mad than scared, if you asked me. Sharp little teeth showing, fur prickling, tail twitching, ball gown in a terrible state. Her rhinestone crown was slipping down over her right eye, but the left one was staring straight at me, black as a gun barrel and not near as friendly.

"She looks like Curious George, don't she, Jim? Just exactly like Curious George."

"Except for the skirt."

"Come on down, little monkey. You want a banana? We got plenty bananas at our house."

"She don't know what you're saying, Mary Al. She's just a dumb animal."

"Shh! You'll hurt her feelings."

"Oh, for crying out loud . . ."

"Run home and get me some bananas, Jim Junior."

"I ain't leaving you here. If that monkey decides to come down and bite you, I'm the one Mama's gonna yell at."

"Well, you stay here, then. I'll get 'em."

Mary Al was off like a shot.

I guess I could have followed her home and called the pound like I meant to in the first place, but that monkey's eye was still trained on me and somehow I couldn't move. Besides, it wasn't like I had much else to do. There weren't but three or four dirt clods left to throw on old Ranger, and after that, just a big fat stretch of nothing.

If Danny'd been here, there'd be a million things. We could throw the ball around or walk down to the U-Totem and play Freako-Maniacs or see if we could collect enough soda cans to buy a couple of movie tickets, if there was anything good on over at the Triangle. Mostly they just had second-run stuff there, which was why you could get in for a dollar fifty, but sometimes they played these great old horror flicks—*Doctor Blood's Coffin* or *The Old Dark House*. Or *The Monkey's Paw*—that was a really cool one about this hairy little shriveled-up hand that put a curse on everybody who touched it.

"What are you looking at?" I muttered.

The gun barrel didn't even blink.

Lord, but it was hot. I wiped the sweat out of my eyes and looked around for Mary Al, but there wasn't any sign of her yet. Or of anybody else, far as I could tell. The playground swings hung limp as old lettuce. Every toddler with a grain of sense was home watching Big Bird in air-conditioned comfort. Waves of heat rippled up from the asphalt on Gilbert Street, turning the mansion all shimmery in the distance, like it was made of smoke.

Course we'd always figured it was haunted. Not much point to it, otherwise. Nobody lived over there but old Mrs. Monroe, who was about a hundred and forty and never went anywhere. Danny claimed it was because her dead husband wouldn't let her leave. She'd slipped roach poison in his poached eggs, you see, so then the old man put a hex on her to get her back. And now she couldn't die, even if she wanted to; she was just over there getting older and older and her skin was all shriveled up and her nose was rotting off and she smelled like that dead rat we found by the drainage ditch last spring.

That was Danny's theory, anyhow, and I figured it was as good as any, but Mama said no, Mrs. Monroe was just a sad old lady with problems like everybody else, and we knew better than to talk such trash.

Well, I felt pretty low then. Truth was, I did know better. Me and Mary Al used to watch for the old girl when we were little, back when that big black gate with the capital **M** would swing open and she'd go sailing out through it in her long black Cadillac with the bald-headed chauffeur driving. Sometimes he'd take her over to the Cut 'n Curl where Mama works part-time, so Mrs. Monroe could get her hair washed and set in those funny-looking flat finger waves that Mama calls marcel. She was just a little bit of a thing, Mama said—a bony little white-headed bird of a lady, perched up under the big bonnet dryer. Might have been anybody's grandmother, only richer.

But it was the rich part Mary Al liked best. She was all the time playing Mrs. Million Dillion, prissing around the house in Mama's old party dresses and cast-off high heels, ordering up room service on the toy phone with the blinking eyes. One time she even tied our beat-up red wagon onto my bike and tried to get me to wear a cap and haul her around the block, but I said no. Good Lord.

And then about three years ago the big gate stopped opening. We didn't know why, exactly. But after that Mrs. Monroe never would leave the place anymore, not even for a permanent wave.

Well, Mama went to worrying then. She gets real attached to all her customers. She says that beauty is more than skin deep, which is why you always feel so much better after you get your roots touched up. So she called over to the mansion and asked could she help out, and they said sure, come on. And ever since then, she'd been going over there to take care of the old lady's hair and fingernails and such. Once a week, rain or shine.

At first Mary Al was all in a sweat to go with her, but Mama said no, Mrs. Monroe's nerves wouldn't stand company. But she promised to tell us about everything she saw, and we held her to it. "Tell! Tell!" Mary Al would holler, as soon as Mama walked in our door. And so she would—all about crystal chandeliers and stained-glass saints on the ceiling and marble floors even in the toilet.

I mostly liked to hear about the creepy parts, myself, like the dead man's boots—Mr. Monroe's, that is—that were still standing next to his bed right where he left them the night he went to sleep and never woke up. He's buried just out back there with a whole bunch of other Monroes. Well, not buried, exactly, because the ground's so mushy in spots around here you can't hardly plant anybody in it for fear of their floating right back up. So what they did, they put 'em in these little stone houses—crypts is what they're called, just like on that television show. Got stone lions guarding the gates and stone angels stabbing snakes up top and I don't know what all. And sometimes our daddy—he used to work over there on the roof repairs and gutters and such before he hurt his back—sometimes he'd make up stories about eyes peeking out or doors creaking open or maybe an arm or a leg that might move just the teensiest bit when nobody was looking.

Course Mary Al was always more interested in the girl stuff, like the nursery with the old-fashioned toys and the baby clothes laid out so neat and pretty, even though most of the kids they were meant for were long since laid out themselves. And we neither of us ever got tired of hearing about the old playhouse that was built to look like a miniature castle, sitting off by itself on its own little island in the private lake behind the mansion. Lake Luly, Mama told us it was called, after old lady Monroe herself—she was Luly Kate Meadowsweet before she got married. It used to be a cypress swamp with alligators and all until they cleaned it out in her honor. Now, that was a shame in my book. You just don't hardly get to see alligators in town anymore. But that little castle was something, all right. I'd caught a glimpse of it myself a time or two from our attic window when the light was just right. But I couldn't tell much about it, really. I asked Mama how the Monroes ever got over there, but she didn't know. Daddy said he sort of recollected there used to be a bridge in the old days, but that was gone now. Far as he could see, there wasn't any way to get across anymore—neither bridge, nor boat, nor wings to fly.

I was still half staring at the old place and half watching my back for monkey bullets when Mary Al showed up with the bananas. There was three of 'em left in the bunch that Mama had bought at Piggly Wiggly the week before— kind of on the soft side now and generally brownish and pitiful-looking.

"What took you so long?"

"I was only gone five minutes."

"Well, never mind. Give 'em here."

"No way! It was my idea! Here, little monkey, look what I got for you." Mary Al peeled a banana back halfway and lifted it as high as she could. "Don't you want a nice ba—"

It was gone before her tongue was done waggling. One long skinny tail looped around a branch, one long skinny arm swooped down, and Mary Al's three was down to two.

"—nana?" she finished.

I swear that monkey was grinning.

CHAPTER three

"What we need is a trap," I said, mostly to myself.

But Mary Al's eyebrows puckered up. "What kind of trap?"

"You know, like the one Daddy built for those coons that kept getting in the garbage last year. That ain't still out in the carport, is it?"

"You want me to go look?"

"Naw, you'll never find it. I b'lieve Mama chopped it up for kindling, anyway. But we might still have one of them big rat traps under the back porch—"

"We can't use that!" Mary Al looked like she was gonna bust out crying again. "That'd hurt her, Jimmy! That'd break her legs!"

"Okay, forget it. I was just thinking out loud, is all—"

"That'd smash her bones all to pieces!"

"Calm down, Mary Al, we ain't gonna hurt her. I'll tell you what we'll do—we'll get a big sack and put the banana in there, and when she goes inside for it we'll just grab it up and close it real quick. How's that?"

I thought it was a pretty good plan, myself, but Mary Al kept shaking her head. "It'll be too dark. She'll be scared."

"Aw, shoot, monkeys ain't scared of the dark."

"How do you know?"

"Well, because—because they come from the jungle, right? It's dark as all get-out in there. That's how they like it."

"You're just making that up."

"Oh, for Pete's sake, Mary Al, you got any better ideas? 'Cause if you don't, either go get me a sack or just forget the whole thing, and I'll call the pound like I should have done in the first . . . Oh, come on now, don't cry. There ain't nothing to cry about—"

But it was too late. Mary Al had crumpled herself into a sweaty little ball of misery down amongst the tree roots that poked up out of the ground there like old gray grand-daddy fingers. "If you call the pound they'll p-put her to s-s-sleep," she sobbed into her lap, "and she'll be d-dead like R-r-ranger. . . ."

Well, that tore me up, her bringing in my dog like that, who was worth a hundred little rat monkeys any day. I gritted my teeth. "Stop that now, ain't anybody else gonna be dead. Come on, Mary Al, please don't cry."

She kept right on, though. Looked like she just couldn't help it. And I didn't know what to do for her, so I was just sort of squatting there beside her, patting her shoulder and wishing I was somewhere more cheerful, like jail, when I noticed old Curious Georgina starting to get restless. She was moving back and forth on the branch up above us, making these little bitty chirping sounds in her throat. Looking *worried*, for crying out loud.

I know this sounds crazy. I mean, forget the dress, this is an actual monkey I'm talking about, banana breath and all. But there she was, shaking her head at us and pacing that branch like an anxious relative on one of them hospital shows. Mary Al didn't see her—or hear her neither, what with the din she was making. But I kept my eyes peeled now. I didn't hardly breathe, just held still and watched while that monkey sweated and stewed and got so bothered that finally she couldn't stand it, she climbed down the tree trunk, over my knees, and right onto Mary Al's shoulder.

I swear.

To Mary Al's credit, she didn't lose her head. Her eyes got big, sure, but she didn't pass out cold or scream bloody murder or jump anywhere near as high as I would have, if it was *my* neck that little stinker was breathing down. No sir, all she did was lift her chin and give a kind of gasp—"Hoh!" is how it sounded—while the monkey made herself right at home on her collar, chittering into Mary Al's ear and fiddling with her ponytail, like you see 'em do on the nature channel when they're hunting for cooties.

Mary Al, meanwhile, had stopped blubbering. It was

the shock, I guess—knocked the tears clean out of her. You never saw a kid go dry that quick. Which ought to have pleased me, I know.

But what I heard myself saying next was "Keep crying, Mary Al! Don't stop now! Long as she thinks you're sad, she'll stay!"

Because it had come to me, you see, what was going on here. That monkey was acting exactly like old Ranger used to when one of us would get hurt or something. He just couldn't stand it, was the thing. He'd come and lick your face till it was all slobbery and start whimpering like *he* was the one with the bloody nose or whatever and just drive you generally crazy with sympathy, till you had to laugh or chase him off, one. He flat could not take crying. And here it turns out this monkey was exactly the same!

Luckily Mary Al had her wits about her—she is pretty smart for seven, even though you wouldn't know it to look at her—and she understood me right off and went to wailing again. You should have seen her, sniffling and moaning and carrying on, and all the time her blue eyes sliding my way, just as sparkly as you please. If I'd had an Academy Award handy, I'da give it to her.

Me, I was the coach. "All right, now, you're doing just fine. But not so loud—ease up a little. . . . Okay, that's it. . . . You can pet her some, I guess. Real soft, that's the way, see how she lets you? Easy, easy. . . . See if you can stand up now, Mary Al. Take it real slow. . . . We got to get her back to the mansion."

"Aw, Jimmy, can't we take her home? Look how sweet she's being! Just for a little while?"

"No, ma'am, no way. Mama'd have a fit. She don't even allow dogs in the house, remember? Come on, now, real easy. . . . That's right. That's good. . . . Just follow me. . . ."

It took some doing, but we did it. Got her all the way out the park and back across Gilbert Street, once we'd waited for the traffic to die down. Mary Al doing her sad routine all the way, and that monkey sticking to her just like Velcro. Then up the wide stone driveway all the way to the M-crowned gate—big and black and closed, as usual, keeping Monroes in and un-Monroes out.

"Should we climb it, like them girls did?" Mary Al wanted to know.

I shook my head. "Wouldn't seem very polite, us coming in like burglars."

"Well, what then?"

I looked up above me and saw what appeared to be an old intercom—a rusty metal box with a circle full of dots in the middle. There was a little black button underneath, doorbell-style. I took a deep breath and pushed it.

Nothing happened.

"Maybe we ought to go around back, like Mama does," said Mary Al. She was thinking of the service entrance, which was how Mama got in for her hair work. But she always drove—it's about a million miles around there, what with the lake and all—and here we were on foot and with this furball.

"Naw," I said. "It's too dang hot." I punched the button again, longer and harder this time.

Still nothing.

"Maybe Miz Monroe ain't home," said Mary Al.

"Maybe she's dead," I muttered. "Maybe the brat grandkid's really an ax murderer, and she chopped her up and fed her to the gators."

Mary Al's eyes got big. "She did not. Mama says they ain't got gators anymore."

I leaned in close to her ear. "That's what they'd like you to think," I whispered, and I smiled my famous dead-eye smile, creeps her out every time.

Well, I was only teasing, is all, but I guess God was listening and decided to punish me for my meanness. Because no sooner were the words out of my mouth than here came the most hellacious noise you ever heard—a squealing, crackling, eardrum-ripping kind of a *skreeek* from out of that old metal box, made me jump about a mile.

And then nothing.

Mary Al tugged on my arm. "Jim Junior?"

"What?"

"This monkey just peed on me."

I can't say as I blamed her—the monkey, I mean. I'm

telling you, that noise was *loud*. "Well, what do you want me to do about it?"

"Let's go home, Jimmy. Can't we just go home?" Mary Al's eyes were starting to fill up for real again.

But I figured we hadn't come this far for nothing. Besides, that godawful racket must have meant something. Maybe they could hear us now, up at the house. I punched the button one more time. "Is anybody home?" I yelled into the squawk box. "We got your monkey out here!"

Still no answer but a solitary cricket, chirping for rain.

Well, by now I was sick to death of the whole thing and flat out of ideas, to boot. I just stood there like a piece of cheese for a couple minutes, and then I gave up. "Come on, then," I told Mary Al, and I turned around and started back toward Gilbert Street—

When all of a sudden there was a loud *click* behind me, and that big black gate started to swing open.

CHAPTER four

Well, *swing* ain't the word, exactly. I guess nobody'd thought to put an oilcan to that gate in the last three years. It made near as much noise as the intercom had, creaking and scraping and carrying on, sounded like something out of *Night of the Living Dead*. I swear, old Danny would've loved it.

Course if Danny was telling this, I guess he'd spruce it up some. He'd probably put in a little thunder and lightning right about here and a whole lot of other gruesome things. Plus maybe he'da left in the alligators. But Danny was halfway to Albuquerque by now, and the sky was just as blue as ever.

"Well, come on then," I said to Mary Al, once that gate had done *skreeking*. And we gritted our teeth and walked on through.

We didn't stick to the big circle driveway but struck out straight across the front lawn, wider'n any football field and twice as long. I was sweating something terrible.

Craggy old oak trees hung over our heads in double rows, made it feel even hotter, somehow. Looked like lined-up widow ladies watching us, with moss shawls drooping off their shoulders. It's not so gloomy through there in the springtime, when the azaleas are blooming and all, but now there was nothing but jungly green leaves and spiky green grass and squat little mounds of crawfish mud all over the place, which we had to watch out not to trip over. Kind of cheered me up to see 'em, same as home. I guess a crawfish don't discriminate between rich yards and poor ones; he just goes ahead and sets right up, regardless.

So anyhow we went on across there, sweating and hopping over them little mud houses and neither one of us saying a word. And by the time we finally made it to the big front steps, my heart was pounding pretty good, thunder or no.

"Jeez Louise," Mary Al muttered, and the monkey shook her little furry head like she couldn't believe it, either.

They were just *so* big, was the thing. I mean, close up like this. If we'd climbed a durn beanstalk, we couldn't have found steps any bigger. There were two sets of 'em, split right down the middle, curving up past a fine white fountain. And ten or twelve fat stone turtles all around that, spitting water just as high as you please. And then a whole row of king-size pillars, like old Samson's chained to in the Bible pictures, propping up one humongous front porch. Bigger'n any porch ever dreamed of being. Course it didn't have any screens to it, so I doubt the family got to sit there much, mosquitoes being what they are. Which seemed like a real waste to me. Why, you could've put half of Hardin County on that porch and still had room for your trampoline.

And you think the *porch* was big? Shoot. It was nothing to the house behind it. I never saw such a stack of bricks. Three stories high and then some, with a front door wide enough to drive a forklift through, and more windows than you could count, and balconies hanging on half of 'em. And chimneys? Come on. It don't get cold enough down here in ten winters running to keep all them suckers in business.

"I guess whoever built it was from out of town" is what I was about to say.

Only right then the burglar alarm went off.

BOOEEP! BOOEEP! BOOEEP! BOOEEP!

I told you it was a bad day.

BOOEEP! BOOEEP! BOOEEP! BOOEEP!

Lord have mercy. At this rate we'd be stone deaf before lunch. I clapped my hands over my ears and looked at Mary Al, who was froze up stiffer'n a Popsicle. "Don't just stand there!" I told her. "Run!"

Wasn't any choosing to it, really. I went one way, Mary Al went another, and the monkey went purely crazy. Jumped off Mary Al's shoulder and started screeching and hollering and tearing around like . . . well, like a monkey, I guess. Some kind of wild jungle animal. Which is what she was, sure, but up till now she hadn't been quite so obvious about it.

BOOEEP! BOOEEP! BOOEEP! BOOEEP!

"Get her, Jimmy! She'll run away again!"

"I ain't gettin' her. You get her! You're the one she likes!"

BOOEEP! BOOEEP! BOOEEP! BOOEEP!

Now the monkey was lunging right toward the white fountain and landing on a stone turtle's back. Now leaping to the next turtle, and the next one, and the next, till I was dizzy just watching her.

All around the mulberry bush, the monkey chased the—

BOOEEP! BOOEEP! BOOEEP! BOOEE—

Then all of a sudden, dead silence.

It was like some huge invisible finger had punched the mute button on the entire planet. Not a car honked, not a bee buzzed. Even the birds had stopped singing. For a good ten seconds every one of us—including the monkey—was stock-still in that big empty quiet.

And then the front door opened, and a giant stepped out.

Well, he *looked* like a giant, anyway.

"It's the bald-headed chauffeur," I heard Mary Al whisper.

And sure enough, it was.

He was way taller than I remembered—but then naturally he'd always been sitting down when we'd seen him driving. And he was wider, too—maybe three hundred pounds, though I'd lay odds most of that was muscle. Plus he was balder, and madder, and much meaner-looking, and just altogether scarier in general.

Nothing missing but the *Fee fi fo fum*.

He stood there for a minute, not making a sound. Looking us over real cool. Until finally when I couldn't stand it any longer, I cleared my throat and spoke up.

"We were just trying to bring you your—"

But the big man shook his head and put up his hand, like he was telling me to stop. So I stopped. Believe me, I stopped. And then he looked at the monkey, and she looked at him, and he lifted up both hands and clapped two times.

And durned if old Georgie didn't jump right off her turtle and go scrambling straight up to *his* shoulder!

It was kind of irritating, to tell you the truth. Looked like me and them screechified girls at the park were the only ones she wasn't friends with. But shoot, what did I care? Good-bye and good riddance. It was over, that was all that mattered.

"Well, I guess we'll be going now," I said, since it didn't look like anybody else was gonna take up the slack, conversation-wise.

But for the second time, the man put up his hand. *Stop,* he was telling me again.

So I stopped. But why? And why the sign language?

He gestured toward the open door. *Come in.*

"Come inside my parlor," said the spider to the fly. . . .

"No, thanks, that's okay, our mama's prob'ly wondering where we are by now and—"

Stop! said the hand. It looked louder this time. And *Come in* was practically a shout.

I opened my mouth to say no again, but Mary Al poked her elbow in my ribs. "Maybe we could run in for just a minute."

"What?" I couldn't believe my ears. "Ten minutes ago you were begging to go home!"

"Well, I know, but . . . well, we're here now, ain't we? And they're our neighbors and all. Mama knows the old lady real good."

Neighbors, nothing. She was dying of curiosity, that was what was wrong with her.

"Ain't nobody gonna bother us, Jimmy."

I was speechless. Hadn't she ever seen a horror movie? *No, you fool, don't go in that old dark house at midnight on Friday the thirteenth with all the fuses blown.* . . .

"I swear, Mary Al—"

Come in, said the hand.

"Well, I'm going," she said. And she was gone.

CHAPTER *five*

Well, shoot. I had to follow her. What else could I do?

The big guy knew it, too. He never moved a muscle while Mary Al darted past his knees and disappeared in the house. He just stood there staring at me, waiting.

So I held up my head and swallowed my spit and climbed them big steps and went on in.

First thing I did when I got inside was run right smack into Mary Al.

"Oof!"

"Watch it!"

"Watch it, yourself!"

She had stopped there, same as me, trying to get a bead on the place. It was dark as a tomb after all that noonday sun. And then little by little it started to come clear. . . .

"Ooh-ee," said Mary Al. Which pretty much summed it up.

We were standing in a huge hallway on a black-and-white checkered floor—made me feel like somebody might come along and king me. Big gloomy pictures looking down at us on either side. There was dark wood on all the walls, and crystal lights burning way up high, and a good many double doors, most all of 'em shut. But we didn't have much time to wonder what was behind 'em, because the big guy had come in with the monkey, and now he was leading us along, sweeping his arm ahead of us to show the way. His boat-size black tennis shoes might just as well been cat's paws, for all the sound they made.

We followed him down the main hall and another that branched off it and then up some twisty stairs and around a corner. And all the time we were getting to wherever it was we were going, we could hear a sort of muffled banging—not like hammering, exactly, more like a bass drum or a battering ram or one of them big pile drivers: *BAM!* and *BAM!* and *BAM!*

"You hear that?" Mary Al whispered. Her eyes were wide as dinner plates, now that she'd got us into this mess.

"Prob'ly just old Mr. Monroe trying to get out of his coffin," I whispered back.

She punched me in the arm. "No, it ain't—" she started. Only just then we come up on another pair of doors, and old Ton o' Fun stopped, so we did, too.

The *BAM!*s were a good bit louder here—no question we were close on 'em now. They kept right on when the big guy knocked three times.

"Is that you, Jasper?" a female voice called.

I said to myself, *Jasper?* But I guess that was his name,

all right. Because now he was opening the doors, and we were walking into another room. And it was big, naturally, like everything else in this place, and full of fine pictures and things—flowers and birds painted every which away on the walls, and statues in the corners, and a grand piano, and the prettiest gold harp you ever seen.

Funny thing, though. Even with all that stuff, this room had an empty feeling to it. Some kind of lonesome cold inside those walls. Course the drapes were drawn, and the AC was cranked up so high, you could've stored meat. But it was more than that, too—something missing in that room. I'm not sure there's even a word for it. You just couldn't picture your mama ever kicking off her shoes in there, let alone asking your daddy to rub her feet.

And in this whole world, you never saw a room that was so much like the person standing in it.

Mrs. Million Dillion herself, is who I mean. Old Luly Kate Meadowsweet Monroe, in the flesh.

She was over by one of the long tall windows, looking out through a slit in them heavy drapes. Had her hand holding 'em back just a little, so the sunshine fell across her face in bars. I couldn't see what she was looking at right then, but I can tell you this much: no hard-timer in the state penitentiary up at Big Spring ever seemed any sadder about his view.

But as soon as she noticed us standing there with the monkey, she went all stiff and careful. Looked like she even got taller, if that was possible. Not that she was all

that tall to start with. If Jasper had turned out bigger than
I'd pictured, Mrs. Monroe was way littler, in actual inches.
But she was tall on the *inside,* if you know what I mean.
Like she ought to be sitting on some throne. I could feel
old Mary Al just dying to curtsy.

"So," said Mrs. Monroe, "the Prodigal returns."

Except didn't that story have a *happy* ending? Because
you sure couldn't tell it from the old lady's face. "Wherever
did you find her, Jasper?"

But Jasper was shaking his head now, and waving
toward us, and talking up a storm with them big hands of
his. Mrs. Monroe just stood there watching him till he was
done. Then she said something in a low voice—I caught
the words *lock* and *cage*—and he nodded like he understood,
so I guess he wasn't deaf or anything. And then he took
the monkey away somewhere and closed the doors behind
him, and me and Mary Al were left all alone with the lady.

She walked over our way now, holding out her hand
real formal. "So I understand it's you two I have to thank?"

"No, ma'am," I said. But my voice crimped up on me
when I shook her hand—which was ice cold, and no
wonder—so I cleared my throat and tried again. "I mean,
you don't have to thank *me.* It was Mary Al here that
caught her. Them girls you invited over chased her clear
to the park."

"And you are—?"

"James Henry Harbert, Jr. Our mama's the one who
fixes your hair."

The old lady actually halfway smiled at that. "Why, you don't say! You're Maggie Harbert's children?"

"Yes, ma'am."

"Well, my goodness. I didn't realize you'd grown so!"

"I'll be turning twelve next December."

"Is that right?" Mrs. Monroe appeared to think this over some, then turned to Mary Al. "And what about you, Miss Harbert? How long have you been taming wild beasts?"

I figured Mary Al would either bust with pride at being called "Miss" or fall down dead from shyness. But she didn't do either one. She just stood there, serious as nails, and said, "All my life."

I stared at her like she'd lost her mind. But Mrs. Monroe, she just nodded and said, "Is that right?"

"Yes, ma'am," said Mary Al. "I found a baby bird fell out of a tree when I was four and a half. We fed him mashed-up cutworms in an eyedropper. And once I taught a lizard how to whistle."

"Oh, for Pete's sake—" Well, *somebody* had to stop her. "He was only puffing out his throat the way they all do."

"He wasn't, either. He could whistle the entire first half of 'Here Comes the Bride.' "

"Good Lord," I muttered.

"Go on," said Mrs. Monroe.

"And we used to have a cat scratched everybody in the family 'cept me, and once I nearly caught a raccoon.

And Ranger always howls along when I sing to him—"
Mary Al broke off there, and looked at me, and hung her
head.

"Ranger?" asked Mrs. Monroe.

"He was our dog," I said. I couldn't say the rest of it.
The "was" was bad enough.

But Mrs. Monroe said, "I see." And then for a moment
there wasn't a sound—

Well, except for that everlasting *BAM! BAM! BAM!*
But that had been going on so long that I'd sort of got
used to it.

Only now . . . well, it seemed like I could halfway hear
another sound with it. Something my ears hadn't picked
up on before. Hard to say just what, exactly. A shorted-
out radio, maybe, or a broken buzz saw—that was probably
all it was. No way it could be some kind of low-down—

Snarling?

The old lady appeared to be listening to it, too. She
had that faraway, ear-cocked kind of look.

"I guess y'all are having some work done," I said, just
to smooth out the hairs on the back of my neck.

"Work?" Mrs. Monroe looked puzzled—like she'd
never heard the word before. Which in her case maybe
ain't as farfetched as it sounds. "What kind of work do
you mean?"

"Well, like, construction work, you know. Getting
your—your roof reshingled, maybe?"

"Oh, no," she said. "Nothing like that."

Like *what,* then? I wondered. Mary Al shot me a look. Lord, I wished I'da never made that crack about the coffin.

But it didn't seem like good manners to ask any more, and anyway right then old Jasper came back. Minus the monkey. He was carrying a pitcher on a silver tray, and some glasses, and some speckledy cookies, and some little blue napkins he'd folded up in fans. I tried to picture him doing it, but I couldn't.

"Thank you, Jasper," Mrs. Monroe said, and then, to us, "Won't you sit down?"

"Oh, no, ma'am. No, thank you, ma'am. We really ought to be going. Our mama—"

"I'm sure your mother won't mind," she said. "You must be thirsty. Please."

Well, shoot. I wasn't all *that* thirsty. And it wasn't as if she was *begging.* I doubt she'd ever begged for anything in her life. But the way that "please" sounded in that big cold room—well, there just didn't seem to be any way out of it, that's all.

So we parked ourselves on some tall white chairs with the hardest bottoms ever invented, and old Jasper handed round the refreshments. Then he left again, and we sat there chewing and swallowing for a while. Mrs. Monroe asked Mary Al if she was looking forward to second grade, and Mary Al said not too much, and blah and blah and on and on like that. And all this time the *BAM!*s kept right on going. But for some reason we all tried to act like we didn't hear a thing, even though that *snarling* sound was getting plainer every minute. Plainer and plainer and—

Good Lord in Heaven.

I choked down my last cookie and stood up and said thanks again, but we really did have to go now. And then I grabbed Mary Al by the hand and started heading for the doors, and I didn't stop to breathe till we were home.

Because what we'd heard back there hadn't been any buzz saw. Or bass drum. Or battering ram.

It was something half-wild beating on its cage door and hollering *"LET ME OUT!!!"*

CHAPTER six

That night we had a thunderstorm would have satisfied even Danny. One of them big old frog stranglers blowing down from Diboll or some such, cracking and booming and black as Judgment Day.

"Y'all don't answer that phone!" Mama hollered from the kitchen, when it rang the first time.

"Why not?" asked Daddy.

We were sitting in the TV room, eating nachos and watching a rerun of one of our favorite shows, "Saltwater Fishing with Paw Paw and Bob."

"Because lightning could strike a pole and then travel right straight through the wires. I saw it on 'Live at Five.' It killed that poor man in Port Arthur not two weeks ago."

"Oh, now, Mama." Daddy rolled his eyes at me. "That was just a freak accident. Odds against it must be eight or nine million to one." And he started to reach for the phone, but Mama came charging in and practically sat on it. There was flour on her sweatshirt and in her hair; made her look unstrung.

"No, sir, don't you touch it! I'm not taking any chances with this family. Whoever it is can just call back, that's all."

I groaned. "But what if it's Danny, Mama? He might be on a pay phone or something. He promised me he'd call from the road somewhere."

"He can call back, James Henry. Just as soon as this storm blows over. We don't want lightning striking Danny, either, now do we?"

Well, personally I was more than willing to risk it, but Daddy was shaking his head at me and giving me that little half smile and his *No sense fighting her on this one, son* look. So I heaved a sigh and covered my ears till the ringing finally stopped, and Mama said, "Okay, then," and went back to her baking.

"If we just had one of them—" I started to grumble, but then I stopped myself. If we just had one of them answering machines like everybody else in the world, we'd at least know who it was, was what I was about to say. But that would have made Daddy feel bad. He hadn't been able to work much since he took that fall last December, when he was putting a new roof on our carport and his ladder broke. It hurt his back pretty bad, and there wasn't any insurance or anything, so sometimes he gets kind of down about bills and such.

"If we had one of what, son?"

I scrambled around in my brain for an answer. "One of them—them sailfish like old Paw Paw's got there. If we had one of them, we could get it mounted and hang it right over the fireplace."

Daddy raised his eyebrows and looked up at what was hanging there now. It was a poster of a bunch of long-legged pink birds that Mama'd picked out over at the Art Mart. She'd spent all one Saturday framing it herself. "You really think she'd let us?" he whispered.

I had to laugh at the look on his face. "Well, I guess we'd have to catch the fish first."

Lightning flashed again. *Boom!* went the thunder. Rain-drops beat on the windows, heavy as fists.

Mary Al cuddled up close to Daddy and tugged on his sleeve. "Can the lightning come through the electric wires, too, and blow up the television?"

"I seriously doubt it, sweetheart." Daddy traced the worry creases on her forehead with his thumb. "We're safe as we can be. But don't go putting that idea in your mother's head." And he chuckled some, and handed her a nacho, and went back to watching Bob catch a speckled trout.

Mary Al was still frowning, though, even while she chewed. Looked like her head was just full up with catas-trophes. She'd been like Mama that way ever since Daddy's accident. I expected she'd start in on tornadoes next—she'd been after me for months now to help her dig a storm cellar like she saw in that *Twister* movie. But what she said was, "Jimmy? Do you think Jasper put that monkey in an inside cage or an outside cage?"

I shrugged. "Shoot, Mary Al, I don't know." I didn't *want* to know, either. If I never heard another word about that monkey and that whole creepy place over there, it would be just fine with me.

But Mary Al wouldn't let up. "Because I was just thinking, if it's an outside cage, that rain could blow right through the bars."

"Well, that's no worse than sitting in a banana tree, is it?"

"And if them bars are made of metal, well, that draws lightning, don't it?"

"For Pete's sake, Mary Al, would you just shut up about the monkey? I'm sick of that stupid monkey."

"She ain't either stupid. And you ought not say shut up."

"Oh, for crying out loud—"

"Stop teasing her, Jim Junior."

"I ain't teasing her, Daddy, I'm just—"

Bbrring! went the telephone. *Bbrring! Bbrring!*

Well, we *all* shut up then and stared at the durn thing, while Mama came in with her hands on her hips and stared at *us*.

"Don't even think about it," she said.

Bbrring! Bbrring! Bbrring! Bbrring! Bbrri—

She stood right there until it stopped again.

"I know it was Danny," I muttered, when she'd gone back to the kitchen. "He *promised* he'd call."

"He'll call back," said Daddy. "Storm'll pass before you know it. Look here, son, extra cheese on this one. Has your name on it."

But I said no thanks and got up and looked out the window. The night was still wild as ever. Lightning lit up the side yard, bright as day. For just a split second I could make out the tallow tree, thrashing around in the wind, bending all but double over Ranger's grave.

I hated to think of him lying out there in that mess. He never could stand the rain. Used to be, on a night like this, I'd sneak him up to my bedroom in the attic. Mama would have had a fit if she'd known about it. But he was always good as gold, never even made a sound.

It thundered again, and the window went dark.

"I bet that monkey's scared," said Mary Al.

I gritted my teeth. Not *that* again—

But Daddy put his arm around her. "Listen here to me, Mary Alice. Don't you worry about that monkey. She comes from the *rain* forest, remember? I bet you anything this is her favorite kind of weather."

Mary Al wiped her nose on her sleeve. She looked real hard at Daddy to see if he meant it. "You think?"

"Yes, ma'am. We saw a show about it, remember that, Jimmy? All about the Amazon River. Biggest river in the whole wide world. And where do you think all the water in that river comes from?"

"Rain?" asked Mary Al.

"Absolutely. You talk about rain! Why, this little old storm ain't nothin' to what goes on down there."

Boom! came the thunder, like it was trying to prove him wrong.

Bbrring! went the phone. *Bbrring! Bbrring!*

"Please," I begged as Mama swooped down on us once more. "What if somebody's in trouble or something?"

Daddy'd had enough now, too. "He's got a point, Maggie. Could be some kind of emergency—"

He reached for the phone again, but Mama beat him to it. I think it was the word *emergency* that had turned her pale. "Hello?" she yelled. "Hello?" She was holding the receiver about six inches from her ear, just in case it started shooting sparks, I guess. I wondered what in the world Danny must be thinking.

"It's for me, ain't it, Mama? Let me talk to him. I'll be careful—"

But Mama was shaking her head at me.

It wasn't Danny at all.

"Why, yes, ma'am, Mrs. Monroe, just fine. And how are you?"

CHAPTER seven

It felt just like that time in kindergarten, when Conrad
Smith pushed me off the teeter-totter. Knocked the breath
clean out of me. Why was that old lady with the cold
hands calling? Why couldn't it be Danny, like he promised?

Some emergency. Probably she just wanted to set up
an appointment with Mama to comb her out or something.
Not that I remembered her ever calling our house before.
But I didn't feel like hanging around to hear. I was sick
of this day, anyhow. Just as soon go to bed and have it
over.

I went on upstairs to my attic and sat there for a while,
listening to the rain beat down. It was always loudest up
here, so close to the roof.

Last time we'd had a storm like this, Danny was spend-
ing the night, and we smuggled old Ranger in and sat up
till three in the morning. Danny'd told me the whole plot
of this great story he was writing. It was about this evil
water skier who falls into a nest of water moccasins with

his mouth wide open and swallows all the eggs right when they're hatching.

Course, we kind of had a fight about it. I told him that moccasins don't lay eggs, they hatch 'em inside their stomachs so the babies come out live. But he didn't want to change it. He said nobody knew that anyway, and I said well, they did if they lived in East Texas. And that hurt his feelings some, I guess, because he wouldn't talk about it after that.

I wished I hadn't said anything about the durn eggs.

I got up and found a ballpoint and one of my old notebooks from school.

"Dear Danny," I wrote in it, *"How's* ~~Phenix?~~ ~~Pheonix?~~ *Did you get there yet? I thought you would call tonight but I guess you couldn't. Listen I might be wrong about them snake eggs. If I can save up enough money I can maybe buy me a plane ticket and come see you and you can tell me that story again. It was real good—"*

I tore out the page and wadded it up and tossed it in the trash can. It was a stupid letter. Where would I get money for a plane ticket? What was I planning to do, rob a bank?

I climbed under my covers and tried closing my eyes, but they wouldn't stay shut. Looked like this day wouldn't end, no matter what.

I was still wide awake when Mama knocked on my door.

"You're not asleep yet, are you, Jimmy?"

"No, ma'am."

She came in then and sat on the side of my bed. Didn't say anything at first. Just picked off a few stray dog hairs from the spread and stared at 'em for a minute, till I thought maybe she was fixing to fuss. But I guess she had something else on her mind, after all, because she never said a word about it, just dropped 'em in the trash on top of my durn fool letter.

The rain was still coming down like crazy.

"You're not catching cold, are you, sweetheart?"

"No, ma'am."

"Well, that's a good thing. Summer cold's always the worst." Mama smoothed down that place in my hair where it sticks out so funny in front. A cowlick is what she says it's called. "Weatherman's promising blue skies tomorrow."

My throat had clotted up on me, so I just nodded.

"You, uh, you haven't made any plans yet, have you, son? For tomorrow, I mean."

Oh, brother. What were we gonna do, beat all the rugs or something? I let out a sigh and shook my head.

"Well, good. Because since you haven't, Mrs. Monroe's asked you and Mary Al over to—"

"*Mrs. Monroe?*" My voice came back, and I sat bolt upright, all at once. "You didn't say we'd *go*, did you?"

"Well, of course I told her I'd have to check with you, but I didn't think you were busy—"

"Aw, man—I don't want to go over there again, Mama. That's the weirdest place I ever been. You don't know what it's—well, I know you've been there to work and all, but not since that . . . that *whatever* she is moved in. They had to lock her up, Mama, like some kind of wild animal. She *bit* one of them girls we saw at the park! And the way she was beating on the door and carrying on—well, we *heard* her, Mama. Just ask Mary Al."

"I already did. She seems real anxious to go."

"Oh, for crying out loud—that's just because of the stupid *monkey*, Mama! You know how crazy she is about animals. She don't have a lick of sense when it comes to anything got fur. She already thinks they're best friends or something, her and that stinky little—why, that monkey *peed* on her, Mama, did she tell you that? I bet she didn't tell you that, did she?"

"She didn't have to," said Mama. I swear it looked like she was trying not to laugh.

"Well, I don't see that there's anything funny about it. I mean, come on, Mama, you're the one always worrying about germs and fleas and all! You didn't even allow Ranger in the house! He was my dog, Mama! He was the best dog in the whole world! And now you're telling me to go play with some spoiled-brat rich kid and her *monkey* while my dog's lying out there dead as a mackerel?"

I couldn't talk anymore. It hurt too bad. And I guess I was blubbering some. But Mama was real nice about it, she hugged me and said it's all right, honey, you just let it out. And then she sat there kind of rocking me and patting my back and waited for me to pull myself together.

Well, I did, finally. Felt like I was never gonna stop, for a while there. But after a few minutes I calmed down some. My chest was still doing that jerky thing, though. Kind of screwed up my breathing and all.

"You okay now, sweetheart?"

"Yes, ma'am."

"You sure?"

"Yes, ma'am. I'm sorry I yelled at you."

"No, Jimmy, I'm the one who's sorry. I just wasn't thinking straight. I knew you'd had a bad day, but when Mrs. Monroe called, I figured—well, I thought the change would do you good, that's all. And I suppose I was flattered, too—you should've heard the way she bragged on you and Mary Al! Said she'd never seen children with better manners. I was so proud. . . . And then she just sounded so . . . well, I guess that child's a handful for her, all right. But Lord knows that's not *your* problem. I'll call Mrs. Monroe in the morning and tell her you don't want the job."

I was nearly half-asleep. "What job?" I mumbled.

"Course Mary Al's going to be disappointed. You're right, she's just crazy about that monkey. She was already planning to save up her earnings and buy one of her own.

Lord in Heaven! Can you imagine? But she'll get over that. She's not but seven—I can't have her going over to that big place all by herself, for goodness' sake."

I opened my eyes. "What earnings?" I asked. "What job?"

"Why, the job Mrs. Monroe offered you and Mary Al, sweetheart. Didn't I explain?"

I shook my head. I was sitting up again.

"I thought she was joking at first. 'Tamers'—that's what she said she needed. 'For the monkey or the child?' I asked her, thinking she'd laugh. But she didn't laugh. She got real quiet. And then she said, 'Both.'"

"And she wants to *pay* us?"

"Well, naturally I told her there wasn't any need. I said I was sure my children would be glad to make friends with the little girl—"

"Aw, Mama—"

"But they'd never take money for a thing like that. And then she begged my pardon. She said she hadn't meant to insult me, or you, either. The payment would be just for feeding and exercising the monkey—monkey-sitting, I guess you could call it. She said it was more trouble than Jasper had time for, and you'd be doing her a big favor."

"Monkey-sitting?" No way. It was the craziest thing I ever heard. I opened my mouth to say so, too.

But then my eye fell on that wadded-up letter. "She didn't—she didn't happen to say how much monkey-sitters *make,* did she?"

"Matter of fact, she did. Says she's offering three dollars an hour."

I thought this over. "Split two ways?"

Mama shook her head. "Apiece."

Apiece! Three dollars an hour! I'd never made that much money in my whole life. And even if I just worked a couple hours a day, that would come to—what? Three times two times seven is forty-two, right? Forty-two dollars a week! And with nine weeks of summer left, if I saved every bit, I *might* have enough for that plane ticket. . . .

Mama was studying my face. "You don't have to make up your mind right now, Jimmy. It's awfully late. We'll talk about it in the morning, okay?"

"Yes, ma'am."

"All right, then." Mama stood up. "You get some sleep, sweetheart."

She kissed me good-night and went downstairs.

The rain wasn't much more than spitting now. Thunder grumbled away off far somewhere.

I raised my window shade and looked out past the treetops to the mansion. Late as it was, the lights were burning.

Ghost lights, Danny used to call 'em. He said no matter how many times the old lady switched 'em off, her dead husband flipped 'em back on, trying to spite her out of a good night's sleep.

Course Mama said ghost lights, nothing, they were just

for keeping off burglars, that's all. And Daddy said the real mystery was how they paid the electric.

Me, I wasn't so sure.

I pulled down the window shade and got back into bed.

Three dollars an hour. But was it worth it?

Because any way you cut it, only one thing seemed dead certain.

Somebody over there was scared of the dark.

II

TO THE ISLAND

Next morning the sun was shining just like the weatherman said it would, so I figured I'd go ahead on and try for the money.

Nine o'clock sharp we're climbing them big steps again. Mary Al's nearly fit to be tied, she's so thrilled about this whole monkey deal.

"Hey, Jasper!" she hollered and waved at him, when he opened the front door. "It's us!"

Course he didn't say anything back. Only gave a little nod (like, *Who else would it be?*) and held the door wide to let us pass.

He took us through the house a different way than he'd done yesterday. Down the stairs instead of up, left instead of right—or was it? Maybe we should have dropped one of them trails of crumbs. We passed another hundred or so closed doors, and finally we come up on what looked to be the dining room. Mrs. Monroe was sitting in there all alone, having coffee. She was away down at the end of a table so long, you could land your crop duster on it.

"Good morning," she said. "I'm so glad you could come again. May I offer you some breakfast?"

"No, thank you, ma'am," I said. "We just now ate."

"Are you sure? Jasper makes wonderful French toast."

"Yes, ma'am, I imagine he does." What was she trying to do, fatten us up for roasting? "But we're full up with pancakes already. If it's all right with you, we'd just as soon get right to work."

"Well, of course, if you're sure. And what about your little sister? Are you ready to see your charge, Miss Harbert?"

"Yes, ma'am, I been ready all morning."

Mrs. Monroe smiled a little at that. "Fine, then. Jasper will tell you everything you need to know."

Tell us? How was he gonna tell us? But I figured I'd find out soon enough, so I said, "Thank you, ma'am," once more and got ready to follow wherever the big guy led.

But before we made it even halfway to the door, Mrs. Monroe spoke up again. "Excuse me, children, just one more thing—I don't know if your mother mentioned that my granddaughter is staying with me?"

Oh, Lord, here we go. "Yes, ma'am, we heard she was."

"And I was hoping that—well, that is, if you wouldn't mind—I was hoping that she might sometimes work with you?"

I looked at Mary Al, who looked back at me. Eyes big as them hotcakes we'd swallowed.

"She's your age, James," Mrs. Monroe went on, before I could get a word in. "Eleven last March. And she's expressed some—well, some interest . . ."

I thought about that snarling. Interest in *what*?

"In animals in general," Mrs. Monroe went on, as if I'd asked it out loud. "And in this creature in particular. It was a gift to me, you see, from my—from her father." The old lady cleared her throat, like she'd got something caught there for a second. Then she went on: "But she's had so little experience with—well, with pets and so forth. . . . She and her mother have moved quite frequently in the last few years, so there really hasn't been an opportunity for them to—" She broke off again there and studied the handle of her spoon like it might help her out some way. "I just thought," she said finally, "that it might do her good."

She put down her spoon and folded her hands and looked at me, waiting for an answer.

Well, shoot, what was I gonna say, *Fat chance*? This was my boss here, for crying out loud. *You mind whatever she tells you,* was the last thing Mama'd hollered out our door.

"We'd be glad to have her help," I said, lying like a rug, trying to ignore the pain in my arm where Mary Al was squeezing.

"Fine," said Mrs. Monroe. Sounded like she was having

that trouble with her throat again. "That's just fine, then. Jasper, show these children the way, won't you? You can stop by Miss Joy's room and see if she's ready."

Joy? I looked at the old lady's face. Joy to who? I wondered.

Wasn't anybody about to tell me, though. So I said, "Thank you, ma'am," one more time, and we followed old Jasper out the door and back down the hall and up the stairs again. And all the time I'm trying to brace myself for this bratty rich kid. Because from what Mrs. Monroe said in there—well, the grown-ups could talk all they wanted to about monkey-sitting, but we all knew what the real deal was. The old lady had her a grandkid so putrid that people had to be paid to play with her.

Seemed like we got to her door way faster than I was ready for. Jasper gave us a look, like *Here we go,* and knocked three times.

Nobody answered.

"Maybe she didn't hear you," said Mary Al.

He knocked again, louder this time.

Still no answer.

"Maybe she's in the bathroom," said Mary Al.

Jasper shook his head, then knocked once more: *Bam! Bam!*

"Go away," said a gravelly voice.

The snarler, no question.

"Well," I said, "I guess she don't feel like coming with us today. I guess we'll just have to try again another—"

I was halfway down the hall when Jasper's big hand took hold of my shoulder. Looked like quitting wasn't gonna be one of our options here.

He hauled me back and took up where he'd left off: *Bam! Bam! Bam!*

"GO AWAY!" said the voice. It was practically roaring now. "What are you, deaf or something?"

And then the door slammed open, and we were eyeball to eyeball with the superbrat herself.

"Good God almighty," muttered Mary Al.

She didn't *look* rich. Heck, no. She looked like something that just crawled out of a ragbag, was what, with her dirty old high-tops and ratty blue jeans and raggedy shirt hanging down. Her hair was no more'n a tangle of filthy brown frizz—at least, what I could see of it sticking out from under the hat she'd got pulled down practically to her nose holes. And talk about a hat! Made to look like the top of a wolf's head, it was, with pointy ears and eyes of its own, beady yellow eyes that came together in slits just over the bill—or snout, was more like it, long sharp snout, teeth and all. It snarled at me over the girl's snarly face, ugliest hat I ever did see.

I wondered where I could get me one.

But before I could open my mouth to ask, Mary Al piped up. Trying to show off how brave she was, I guessed, judging from the jut of her jaw and the white of her knuckles on the hand that was still clamped around my biceps. But her voice was right steady, all things considered.

"We've been hired," she announced, "to tame you."

Lord have mercy. The attack of the killer shrimp.

For a second I thought the wolf girl was gonna laugh. Which would have hurt Mary Al's feelings something awful. But she didn't laugh. She just stared, was all, first at Mary Al, then at me, like she hadn't ever seen regular human kids before. And then just when I was right on the edge of thinking of something smart to say—

"I can't *be* tamed," she growled.

CHAPTER nine

"What we *mean* to say," I tried to explain, "is that your grandma hired us to help out with the monkey."

"Big freaking deal," said Miss Joy Monroe. "Like I'm supposed to give a rat's—"

I cleared my throat real loud. "This is my *little sister* here, miss. She's not but seven, for your information."

"Oh, yeah?" The wolf girl made her green eyes go squinty. "And what's your name, little sister?"

Mary Al stood up real straight. "Mary Al," she said, sticking out her chin. "That stands for Mary Alice."

Miss Joy smiled an evil smile. Ain't no other way to describe it. I read about 'em in books, but I never had seen one live. "Well, my name's J.D." She batted her stubby eyelashes. "That stands for Juvenile Delinquent."

I gave her my best dead-eye stare. "So we've heard."

This seemed to please her, more than anything. She turned her creepy green peepers on me. "And what about you, Billy Bob? You in the *#@!-kicking business or what?"

You might as well know right now, I won't be telling you every word she said. Mama don't allow us to talk that kind of trash. Not that I hadn't heard it all over at Danny's on cable TV. But it burned me up, her shooting off her mouth like that in front of Mary Al.

"My name is James Henry Harbert, Jr., and I don't give a hoot in Hades what you think of me. But you mess with my little sister and you'll regret it."

Old J.D. didn't answer right away. Just stood there looking at me, like she was sizing me up for my coffin. And then she snorted. "Lighten up, Jimbo. She's safe till lunch. I already had my breakfast."

I took ahold of Mary Al's arm. "We got no time for this. Come on, Mary Al. Three bucks an hour ain't worth it."

I turned around and started to pull her along with me, but I almost run right slap into Jasper's stomach. I'd forgot all about him, to tell you the truth. He was standing just behind us in the hall, with his big arms folded—looked like that bald-headed guy on the floor-soap bottle.

" 'Scuse me," I said, trying to get by.

Old Jasper didn't budge.

"Aw, come on, Jasper. What do you care if we quit? You and that monkey been getting along fine without us."

Mary Al jerked her arm away from me. "I ain't quitting, Jimmy! That girl don't scare me. We ain't even seen the monkey yet all morning!"

I should've known better than to bring up the dad-blamed monkey.

"Oh, for Pete's sake . . ." There wasn't gonna be any way out of this deal, I could see that right now. Not unless I was ready to *carry* her all the way to our house. I took a deep breath and blew it out real slow. "Well, all right, then. We'll feed it or sit it or whatever we have to do, and then we're going right straight home, you got that?"

Mary Al nodded. "I got it."

The Juvenile Delinquent snorted behind my back. "You tell her, Jimbo."

Even without looking, I could see that evil smile.

I gritted my teeth. "Come on, Jasper. Let's get this over with."

He unfolded his arms then and started leading the way again. Didn't even check to see if the wolf girl was following. This surprised me some, after the way he'd banged on that door. But I figured it was like them Christmas parties Mama gives to pay back all the relatives who've had us over. She says if you invite 'em and they don't show, it still counts.

Well, anyhow, looked like J.D. wasn't coming, and I wasn't about to shed any tears. So we stuck close to Jasper and walked along in peace another mile or so, down and around and right and left again. Until finally we were climbing down a whole different set of stairs, narrower and steeper than any of the others had been.

"Y'all got a cellar down here?" I asked. "Don't it flood every time it rains?"

Jasper shook his head—though to which question, I couldn't tell you. And then we come to the bottom of the stairs, and there was the monkey.

I almost didn't recognize her, without her rhinestones. They'd taken away her crown and her ball gown, too. She was just a little old furball now, not much bigger than a good-size squirrel, staring out at us kind of pitiful through the bars of her cage.

"Hello, little monkey," Mary Al said real soft. "You feeling okay this morning?" And then she tiptoed over just as quiet as you please and reached out one hand, easy like, and the monkey came right to her and started that chittering sound.

Which just goes to show, there ain't no way of telling how a seven-year-old's gonna act. Here I'd thought she'd go charging in there all excited—I mean, she hadn't talked about anything else for the last twenty-four hours. But when she looked back at me and Jasper, her eyes were leaking again.

"She's all locked up," she whispered. "Can't you let her out, Jasper? Please, can't you let her out?"

Jasper looked at her real hard for a minute, like he was thinking it over. And then he nodded.

"Oh, thank you, Jas—"

He held up his hand, telling us to keep still, and walked over to a little cabinet right next to the cage.

It wasn't a *terrible* cage or anything. Pretty good size for just one little monkey. It took up near a quarter of this downstairs storage room. Plus somebody had gone to a good bit of trouble to fix it up. They had put a couple swings in there—like you see in a birdcage, only bigger—and some nice monkey playtoys: a red ball and a plastic mirror and a rubber bunny with a big goofy grin on its face. Had some plants in there, too, to make it feel more like the jungle, I guess. One of 'em was practically a whole little tree.

So, all in all, it was just fine, as cages go—and it was *inside,* too, like Mary Al was asking about before. That monkey'd be safe in here, all right. No storm would ever keep her up nights. Why, there wasn't even a window where the lightning could get through.

Or the sunshine, either. Or the salt breezes blowing up from the Gulf. Or that cheerful kind of twittering when a bird flies by.

But what was I thinking, anyhow? What would a monkey care about twittering birds? It was a perfectly fine cage, anybody could see that.

Still, I was glad to see old Jasper opening the cabinet, and taking out a key, and putting it in the cage lock, and starting to turn—

When all of a sudden that monkey let out a *shriek!*

would've curled your hair and started skittering around the cage like she'd lost her mind for good.

Yeep! Yeep! Yeep! Yeep!

Up and down and sideways and inside out—you never saw anything move that fast. And all the time just a-*screaming* fit to raise the dead.

Yeep! Yeep! Yeep! Yeep!

Well, old Jasper, he wheeled around and stared at us real hot-faced, like he thought *we'd* done something to set her off. But me and Mary Al were just standing there blank as new paper. Which seemed to puzzle him for a second— until his eyes hit on something behind us. His scowl got even scorchier then—I swear, you could almost smell the smoke. And then he raised one long finger and pointed back there, like he was saying, *YOU!!!*

Even before I turned, I could feel the wolf eyes.

CHAPTER ten

Yeep! Yeep! Yeep! Yeep!

"What's wrong with her?" the Delinquent growled. She was standing at the bottom of the stairs, glaring at us.

"Maybe it's the hat," said Mary Al.

For about a quarter of a second, old J.D. looked surprised. Her hand went up to the wolf hat, then dropped away real quick behind her back.

"It's just a hat, that's all. It's not *alive*. What's she think, it's gonna eat her or something?"

Yeep! Yeep! Yeep! Yeep!

"I'd say that's a yes," I muttered.

"She's just such a *little* monkey," explained Mary Al.

"Well, that's just a load of—"

Jasper clapped his hands, making us jump. He pointed to the girl, then to his own head, then swept his arm down and out. Like, *Just take the fool thing off, why don't you?*

J.D. snorted again. "What's wrong with *him?*"

"Not a thing," I answered. Not that I really knew.

But I couldn't just stand there and listen to her bad-mouth old Jasper. "He's telling you to take off the hat, that's all."

She shook her head. "I never take off this hat."

Mary Al gasped. "Not even in the bathtub?"

"Bathtub?" The wolf girl curled her lip. "What's a bathtub?"

Yeep! Yeep! Yeep! Yeep!

Jasper'd had enough. He took a step toward J.D. and pointed up the stairs.

"I ain't going anywhere," she snarled.

Jasper took another step. *Wanna bet?*

Still J.D. stood there sneering, with her hands on her hips. Looked like one of them Wild West showdowns at the movies. With old Sheriff Jasper closing in on the desperado: *It's you or me or the hat, pahdner. One's gonna have to go. This town ain't big enough for the three of us.*

"Just take off the hat!" begged Mary Al. "Before he—before he—"

Yeep! Yeep! Yeep! Yeep!

"Before he what?" the wolf girl growled. "He wouldn't dare. Would you, you big dummy? Come on, I dare you. Old tub o' guts. You think you scare me? You don't scare me. Why, you couldn't even—you wouldn't—don't you *touch* it!" she roared, as he took one last step, and she grabbed hold of her hat with both hands—

But it wasn't the hat he was aiming for. Quick as any quarterback, he scooped up the whole girl like she was an ornery football and carried her, kicking and screaming, to

the top of the stairs. And then he set her down real careful
outside the door—making sure to hold her at arm's length
while he done it, so her claws just scraped the air, not
him—and he closed the door and latched it and climbed
back down.

"Let me in!!!" we could hear her hollering. *"Let me
in!!!"*

Well, the morning improved considerable after that.
Once Jasper got the monkey calmed down. I don't know
how he did it, with all that racket coming from up top the
stairs, but he did. Just walked back to the cage as calm as
you please and opened it and clapped three times, and the
monkey went leaping onto his shoulder like her daddy'd
come to save her at last.

I could feel Mary Al just itching to get her hands on
her, but she had sense enough to wait her turn. So we
stood there watching while Jasper took his time, petting
the monkey real easy and scratching her behind the ears
and making these quiet little clicking sounds with his
tongue. And before too long she had settled down pretty
much to normal.

The banging and hollering went on for a bit more,
while Jasper showed us what we needed to know—where
he kept the rake and all, and how to muck out the old
straw at the bottom of the cage and bag it up and scatter
around the fresh. There was a little sink hid away behind
some boxes, too, where we could wash out the water bowl
and fill it up, and even a pint-sized icebox with monkey

food inside—lettuce and figs and oranges and bananas and broccoli and cauliflower and such. Plus a vase filled with some of them common yellow flowers that'll drive your mama crazy, turning all to fuzz in your grass. I thought for a minute old Jasper had gone over the edge—picking flowers for a monkey, I mean. But it turned out they were for eating, not looking at, because he sprinkled 'em right there in the food tray with all the other stuff.

I figured we were pretty much done then, but Mary Al hadn't even got started. "Do you think she'd let me hold her now, Jasper?"

He started to shake his head.

"Please, Jasper—"

"Let him alone, Mary Al. You can hold her some other day when she knows us better."

Jasper looked at me when I said that, like I'd reminded him of something. And then he let out a sigh and handed us each a fig.

"Thanks," I said, and was just about to pop it in my mouth, when he shook his head again and pointed to the monkey. "Oh," I said. "You mean for her?"

Jasper smiled. Not a big hee-haw grin or anything, but a definite twitching around the mouth corners. And then he nodded.

So we held up the figs, and the monkey eyed 'em for about ten seconds, and then she reached out and took 'em—Mary Al's first, then mine.

It wasn't like that other time at the park, when she

grabbed the banana away so quick. This was more . . .
well, *polite,* if that makes any sense. Something about the
way she was looking at us, maybe—like we weren't the
enemy anymore. And you know, it was funny, but up
close like this, them eyes of hers weren't bullet black at
all. They were more of a brownish color, really, all shot
through with some kind of goldy light.

Not so different from old Ranger's, come to think of it.

Which is maybe why my stomach knotted up so peculiar when Jasper handed her—not to Mary Al—but to me.

I didn't know she'd be so soft.

"Ain't she sweet, Jim Junior? Don't you just love her?
Say something to her! Don't just stand there."

I couldn't think of anything to say. But Jasper was
nodding at me, too, and I figured, well, if *he* can do it. So
I tried making those little clicking sounds with my tongue.
Which sounded kind of foolish to me, but she seemed to
like it pretty well. Next thing I knew, she was chittering
away real cozy on my shoulder and messing around with
my hair.

It tickled some, but not too bad.

"She likes you now, too, huh, Jimmy?" Mary Al was
doing her best not to sound jealous. "I guess she likes pretty
much everybody now."

"Well, maybe not *everybody*," I said. I raised my eyebrows and nodded toward the top of the stairs—

Which is right when I noticed how quiet it was. No
banging, no hollering, no kicking on the door.

I looked at Jasper. "Do you think she's gone?" I was whispering, for some reason.

He followed my eyes, then put a finger to his lips. Listening for wolves, I guess. Then he lifted his hand— *Keep still, you two*—and started climbing the stairs again.

Oh, man. What was the brat kid up to now? Ain't no way she'd give in that easy. Could be she was just sitting there waiting to jump us.

And if she was? Well, then, would it really be her that was locked *out,* or us that was locked *in?*

I held my breath as he reached the top. Lord, I could feel it in my bones. Any second now, he'd throw open the door, and the wolf girl would come howling through. . . .

But he must have been thinking the same thing I was, because he didn't even touch the door, just stood there listening for a minute. And then he shook his head and came back downstairs.

"Is she still out there?" Mary Al whispered.

Old Jasper, he only shrugged.

"Well, what are we supposed to do," I asked, "just *sit* here?"

Jasper didn't bother to shake his head. He walked over to a little beat-up dresser that was standing by the icebox and opened a drawer and took out what looked like an old dog collar and a leash. And then he brought those over and put 'em on the monkey and motioned for us to follow him. So we did—past the cage and in between some more boxes and around one of them fancy wooden screens with a fire-breathing dragon painted on it.

And lo and behold, what I'd thought was a blank brick wall had a door in it, after all.

Well, hallelujah. I started breathing again, while Jasper fiddled with keys. Shoot, I should've known better than to get all stirred up over nothing. That old girl had me so spooked, I was jumping at doodlebugs. Good thing she didn't know it. And she wasn't going to, either, I told myself, as he swung the door open. Not if I had anything to—

"Yeeeiii!" shrieked Mary Al.

"Yeep!" yelled the monkey.

"What took you so long?" asked J.D.

CHAPTER eleven

She'd taken off the wolf hat. Not that it helped much. Even without it, the scowl on her face was still plug-ugly. If Jasper hadn't had such a good grip on the leash, the furball would have been up another tree faster'n you could say monkey stew.

"So what's wrong with her now?" J.D. growled.

Was she kidding? You could all but see the poor critter peeking out from a red hood. *But Grandma, what big teeth you have!*

"She's remembering the hat." Mary Al looked suspicious. "I thought you said you never took it off."

The green eyes went squinty again. "Not unless I feel like it. You got that, baby sister? It's hot out here, in case you didn't notice."

"Who you calling a baby?" Mary Al started in, but Jasper held up his hand. *Enough,* he was saying. *Enough.*

J.D., she just folded up her arms and shrugged her shoulders. Even backed off a step or two, biding her time.

Course I didn't trust her any further'n I could throw her. No telling what kind of devilment she had cooking in that head of hers. I kept my eyes peeled for trouble while Jasper got the monkey settled again, clicking and petting and all of that. He walked her around the yard some, too, like I seen my Aunt Barbara do when little Mollie Ann's got the colic, stroking her back and pointing out birds and flowers and such. And all this time the rest of us just stood there by the door, watching one another out the corners of our eyes and not saying spit. Until—

"You know she cut out his tongue," J.D. muttered.

I stared at her full-out now. *"What?"*

"Shh. He'll hear you."

I lowered my voice. "Who, *Jasper?* What are you talking about?"

Mary Al poked her head in closer. "Somebody cut out Jasper's *tongue?*"

J.D. nodded. "The old lady. My grandmother. She did it."

"She did not."

"Well, not with her own *hands*. Too messy. She hired a renegade doctor to do the job."

"That's a lie," I said. "Don't pay any attention to her, Mary Al. That's the biggest lie I ever—"

"Shh!" said J.D. "Why do you think he never talks?"

"Because—" I began, "because he—"

"Because he can't, that's why. *Ask* him, why don't you? Go ahead."

"I'll ask him," said Mary Al. "Jas—"

"No!" I grabbed her arm just in time. "You can't ask him a thing like that—"

"Why not?"

"Yeah." J.D. went all wide-eyed. "Why not?"

I ignored her and spoke right to Mary Al. "Because it might make him feel bad," I whispered. "It ain't polite to point out what a person's got missing."

"Like your brother's brain," J.D. said sweetly. "He just *hates* when people notice, don't you, Jimbo?"

I wish I could say I had a snappy comeback all ready— I did think of eight or nine real good ones later on, as I recall—but unfortunately at the time my mind was pretty much a blank.

Course Mary Al jumped right in to defend my intelligence. "Nuh-*uh*!" she cried. Which only caused old J.D.'s smirk to shoot up a couple more notches on the snottiness scale.

"Nuh-*uh*?" she mimicked. "Nuh-*uh*?"

I glared at her. "You think you're so smart? You ain't all that smart. Ain't no reason for your grandma to go around cutting out tongues. Why would she want to do a thing like that?"

"So Jasper can't tell anybody her secrets, that's why. You think a guy like that doesn't know where all the bodies are buried around here? The old lady's just making sure nobody else ever finds out, that's all."

Mary Al's mouth dropped open. "*Bodies?* What bodies?"

I rolled my eyes. "I told you not to pay her any mind, Mary Al. She's just trying to scare you."

J.D. nodded. "Yeah, right. Don't listen to me. Maybe I'm just making it all up." She cocked a skinny eyebrow. "Then again, maybe I'm not."

"Oh, for crying out—if Jasper knows all these big secrets, why don't he just write 'em down? Why would he stick around here after she done a thing like that to him? Why don't he just quit and type up the whole shebang and take it down to the police station?"

J.D. heaved a big sigh, like I was the slowest three-year-old she ever run across. "You don't think he *wants* to?"

"Well, why don't he, then?"

J.D.'s voice got even lower. "*Blackmail,* that's why not."

"Blackmail?" Mary Al sounded horrified. She looked at me. "What's blackmail?"

J.D.'s eyes were just green slits now. "Granny's got something on him, is how I figure it. No telling what *he's* been up to. He rats on her, she rats on him. No way he can risk it, that's all."

"Aw, man, that's the craziest thing I ever—"

"Is it?" J.D. whispered. "Just look at him. A big guy like that? He could smush you like a bug if he wanted to."

I looked. At the moment Jasper was plucking a purple

hibiscus blossom and offering it to the monkey and all the time making them little clicking sounds with his—

"Aha!" I said, so loud that everybody—even the monkey—turned around and stared. "Nothing," I called, waving to Jasper, who was looking at me like I'd lost my mind. "Everything's okay now. Everything's just fine. . . ."

"What are you smiling about, Sherlock?" J.D. hissed. "You think you solved some big mystery?"

"One more'n you did." Lord, but this felt good.

"You gonna tell us about it, or do we have to guess?"

"Ain't no guessing to it, if you just use your head. And your *ears* . . ."

Mary Al didn't get it. "Our *ears?*"

"Shh!" said J.D. She screwed up her face, listening.

Click, click, click, click . . .

"Oh," she said. "You mean *that.*"

"What?" asked Mary Al.

"That clicking noise," said J.D. "Big brother here thinks that Jasper couldn't make a sound like that if he didn't have a tongue. Isn't that right, Jimbo?"

"Exactly. And my name is—"

"James Henry Harbert, Jr. I know, I know. And I really hate to disappoint you, Jimmy Hank, but there's a little something you haven't thought of."

"Oh, yeah?" Man, oh, man, how I hated this girl. "You gonna stand there and try to tell me—"

"One word." J.D. leaned in and blew her evil breath right in my face. *"Stub."*

I felt sick to my stomach.

"Stub?" Mary Al repeated. "What's that supposed to—" Her face changed. "Oh, you mean he makes them clicks with the stub of his—*eeyyooo . . .*"

"You got it, babycakes." I swear, there were *sparks* flying out of them green slits now. "Try it yourself, anybody can do it. Just stick the tip of your tongue on the roof of your mouth and hold it real still, see, right there behind that big gap in your front teeth, and then—"

I pulled Mary Al away from her. "Leave her alone. She's only a kid. What are you, sick or something? Talking that crazy talk. You can't prove a word of it."

The wolf girl smiled her poison smile. "Can't I?"

Well, I knew she was bluffing, but just then somebody touched my shoulder from behind, and durned if I didn't jump about a mile. It was only Jasper trying to give me another turn with the monkey—just *startled* me a little, was all—but old J.D. just about passed out laughing. So I didn't feel one bit sorry for her when she pushed in wanting a turn, too, and the monkey got all nervous again and wouldn't let her anywhere near. Served her right, is what I thought, when Jasper handed Mary Al the leash instead. Course Mary Al thought she'd died and gone to heaven, and J.D. tried to act like she didn't care—just stood there watching with her mouth shut tight, for once. But she didn't fool me. I saw how she kept balling up her hands into fists, over and over again. And then while Jasper was helping Mary Al get the leash untangled from an azalea bush, J.D. come up to me and muttered, "You want proof?"

I didn't. Not really. But for some reason I said, "Yeah, sure."

So she said, "Follow me," and we went down a stone walk and under some kind of cement archway and around a big hedge of sweet-smelling yellow flowers—

When all of a sudden Lake Luly spread out before us like a fresh-cut sheet of plate glass, shining so hard I had to shade my eyes. And then I saw it—that little green island, pointing its castle towers at the sky.

"There's your proof," the wolf girl whispered.

CHAPTER twelve

"Proof of *what?*"

J.D. didn't look at me. Her eyes were fixed on the island. "She's hiding something out there."

"Aw, come on. Your grandma?"

"There used to be a bridge. Started right over here—look, you can still see a couple of the old pilings. But she tore it down."

"So? Ain't a crime to tear down a bridge on your own property."

"Maybe not. But why would a person do a thing like that?"

"I don't know. Maybe she just got sick of it."

"Why would anyone get sick of a bridge?"

"Maybe it was falling down or something. Maybe it was dangerous."

"Then why didn't she just fix it?"

"*I* don't know. . . ." My brain was starting to hurt. I stared across the shining water at that patch of green, floating all peaceful away out there in the middle. But no answers stared back. The place was mum as Jasper. "Why don't you ask *her*?"

"I did. You should've seen the way she looked at me."

"How?"

"Like . . . like she was *hiding* something. She didn't want to talk about it, that's for sure."

"Shoot, you can't tell anything from the way a person *looks*. Maybe she had a headache. You take my mama when she gets one of them, you don't even want to be in the same *state*. Looks don't mean nothing. It's what she *said* that counts."

J.D. shook her head. "Yeah, right. Like she's really gonna tell me the truth."

"Well, why wouldn't she?"

J.D. sneered. "What planet you come from? When was the last time a grown-up told *you* the truth?"

I just stared at her. This morning, I thought. Last night. Day before yesterday. My folks might have their faults, but they sure as heck ain't liars.

But J.D. wasn't expecting an answer. She picked up an acorn and sidearmed it into the water. Had a pretty good spin on it for a girl. "I *told* you, she's hiding something out there. You deaf or just stupid? No way she's gonna come right out and *admit* it."

"Okay, suit yourself. What do I know? Your grandma's an ax-swinging psycho chainsaw murderer? Fine with me. Call in the durn Texas Rangers, why don't you?"

"Maybe I will."

"Well, go ahead, then."

"You think I wouldn't?"

"You think I *care*?" Man, this girl was a pain. I started to walk away.

But while she was shaking her fist at me, I happened to notice this little wrinkled Band-Aid kind of half-hanging on one of her knuckles. Not even close to covering the nasty red scrape it was intended for. Probably something she got from banging down some door, I figured. Or picked up in a prize fight somewhere. If it had been Mary Al, Mama'd have that ugly hurt cleaned off and Mercuro-chromed and gauzed up so neat you could bounce a quarter off it. I wondered at Mrs. Monroe not tending to it better. Course maybe it wasn't altogether her fault, seeing as how the kid could've practically been the poster child for Fangs Week on "Wild Discovery." She probably never let the old girl close enough to *see* the scrape, much less tend to it.

Durn Band-Aid bothered me, that's all. I wished *I'd* never seen it.

I kicked at a white rock and turned back around. "Look, just for grins, would you mind telling me what your grandma said when you asked her about the bridge? Her actual *words*?"

J.D. was quiet for a minute, studying my face. Looked like she was trying to decide if I'd be better oven-baked or deep-fried. Then she bit off a hangnail and spit it over her shoulder. "I don't remember her *exact* words. Something about . . . repairs being too expensive, or a waste of time, I don't know. Something lame like that."

"Well, there you go! It was busted, that's all—"

J.D. shook her head again. "You weren't there. You didn't see her face. It was like . . . like I'd *hit* her or something. Socked her in the stomach. You know."

I nodded. Even though I didn't know, really. Socking old ladies is frowned on in my family. But then I remembered who I was talking to. "You didn't—" I tried to think how to put this without starting World War Three. "You didn't *bite* her or anything?"

J.D. rolled her eyes. "No, I didn't bite her. She's about a million years old."

"Just checking. I didn't know you had an age limit."

Her face twitched. "Absolutely. Nobody under two or over two hundred."

"Nice of you to narrow it down." I picked up an acorn of my own and chucked it about twenty yards shy of where hers had splashed.

The wolf girl grinned. An actual grin. For a split second she looked almost human. "Well, I had to draw the line somewhere," she said, firing off another nut herself. "Otherwise it's just work, work, work." *Plop!*

"Wow," I muttered. I couldn't help it. That last toss of hers had practically hit the island. "That's some arm you got."

She shrugged. "It's not bad."

"Not bad?" I handed her another acorn. "Do that again."

"Do what?" She was trying not to smile too big. "You mean this?" She let it fly. . . . *Plop!*

"Good grief—" That one went even further, I swear. "You on a team, or what?"

"Nah." She was like one of them TV ballplayers in an interview after the game, trying to look modest and all. "I never had the time." *Plop!*

"Never had *time?* Man, if I could throw like that . . . Who taught you to throw like that, anyway?"

She shrugged again. "My dad."

"He must be pretty good. What's he do, play for the Astros or somebody?"

I meant it as a compliment, but for some reason J.D.'s grin went sour as month-old milk. "What do you care?" she snarled.

Lord, she was prickly. Must have been an American League fan.

"Who says I care? I was just asking, is all."

"Well, don't ask. You got that, Monkey Boy? For three bucks an hour you can mind your own #*@! business."

It wasn't the cussing that bothered me so much. It was the snotty way she said "three bucks an hour"—like that was something to be ashamed of. I wished I had the money in my pocket so I could throw it at her, but all that was in there was a couple nickels and a Tootsie Roll wrapper. So I just looked at her, cold as freezer burn, and then I turned around and walked away for real.

CHAPTER thirteen

"Dear Danny," I wrote in the notebook, *"I got a job today so I could save up enough money to come see you in ~~Phonex~~ ~~Pheonix~~ but I'm quitting tomorrow so forget it. Turns out there's a monkey over at the haunted mansion and me and Mary Al are supposed to tend to it but that's not the bad part. The old lady has her grandkid staying with her now and you talk about a brat, she's worse than anything you ever made up even including Bloodsucking Hairballs From Hell. I mean the dang monkey has better manners than—"*

"Jim Junior? You up there?"

"Yessir."

"Come down here for a minute, will you, son? I need you to hold this garbage can lid steady while I grease the tracks. Your mama says they're sticking some."

I sighed and put down my pen. "Yessir. I'm coming."

I didn't really feel much like it, though. Sounded like

Daddy was down there fooling with his invention again.
I got depressed just thinking about it. Not that it wasn't
good—it was, it was real good. Mama said it was the
handiest thing she'd ever even heard of. It was this big
wooden box he'd built right there in the middle of our
kitchen, you see, with a door on it so you could put one
of them giant-size garbage cans inside. And then up top,
instead of a regular lid, he'd made this big heavy-duty
cutting board where you could chop up your onions and
carrots and such, and when you were done you just gave
this board a push, and it slid right back along its tracks so
all the little green tops and whatnot you had left over could
just go straight into the trash underneath. I don't know if
I'm explaining it exactly right, but it was a great invention,
believe me.

Anyway Mama loved it, and Daddy got to thinking
he could maybe get one of them patents on it from the
government and prob'ly make a whole ton of money,
which would have helped considerable with the bills and
all. Only trouble was, somebody must have got wind of
it, because it turned out they stole his whole idea and
started selling 'em down at the Shop 'n Swap before he
ever got around to filling out the paperwork. Course Daddy
didn't get all that mad about it, but I never could see why
not. It made me almost sick to think how close we come
to being rich, and only just missed.

Well anyhow I went on down there. Daddy was the
only one in the kitchen. He was working on the box and

kind of mumbling to himself—"Well, shoot, dad-blamed wheel's gone crooked again, ain't it? Gonna have to look for a new one over't Handy Dan. Maybe next time I should—" He looked up and saw me. "Hey, sunshine. Come over here and press hard as you can on this board, will you? I about had it licked, but my back seized up on me."

That was why he was standing sort of crooked, then. "You want me to get you one of your pills?"

"Naw, it'll pass here in a minute. Just hold that board steady, if you will—there you go. That's the ticket. Let me get a little grease in there now. . . . We'll have her sliding smooth as silk time your mama gets home."

"Where is she, anyway?"

"She had to run your sister over to Patty Patrizi's birthday party. Weren't you invited, too?"

"No sir, that's just little kids. I'm a lot older'n all of them."

"Well, sure you are. I don't know what I was thinking. Can't get used to you growing up so fast, I guess. Hand me that rag, will you, son? That's the one. . . . How'd your job go this morning, anyhow?"

Shoot. I knew this was coming. Better just say it straight out and get it over with. "I'm thinking about quitting."

Daddy looked up again. "Quitting? You only just got started."

"I know, but—"

"Your sister still seemed all revved up about it. Couldn't stop talking about that monkey. She behaved herself, didn't she?"

"She was okay. Ain't Mary Al that's the problem."

"Well, who is, then?"

I shook my head. "Aw, man, Daddy, that girl over there—I don't think I can take a whole summer of her. Mrs. Monroe said we were hired to sit the monkey, but that ain't really the deal. And old J.D. knows it, too. Hates it even worse'n I do. She may be a lot of things, but dumb ain't one of 'em."

"So what's wrong with her, then?"

I puffed up my cheeks with air and blew it out real slow. "She's foul-mouthed and stuck up and a liar and mean as a snake. And she *bites,* for crying out loud."

Daddy's eyebrows shot up. "She bite *you?* Or Mary Al?"

"Naw, neither one of us. Just didn't get around to it, I guess."

"I see. . . . What else is wrong with her?"

What else? How much else did there have to be? "I don't know, Daddy—if you could just hear her—ain't nothing *right,* far as I can tell. 'Cept maybe her throwing arm," I added under my breath.

"Her what? Did you say throwing arm?"

I sighed. Just seemed like such a waste. "Crazy girl can really bring it."

"Is that right?" Now Daddy was shaking *his* head. "The apple don't fall far from the tree, I guess. Hand me that screwdriver, will you, son?"

"Apple?" I didn't understand. "No sir, weren't no apples over there. It was nuts we were throwing."

Daddy chuckled. "Just an old country saying, that's all. You know—chip off the old block? Like father, like daughter? That little girl's daddy was the best third baseman I ever saw."

"He was?" Well, I'll be dogged. Looked like I'd been on the right track all along! So what had old J.D. got so riled about, anyway? "He didn't play for the Astros, did he?"

"Naw, this is just high school I'm talking about. But Max Monroe was something, all right. You hit a ball anywhere near him, you just as well go on back to the dugout and have yourself some Cracker Jacks, he's gonna throw you out no matter how fast you run."

"Y'all went to school together?"

"Well, he was a year ahead of me. Ran with a different crowd, mostly. But I knew him to speak to." Daddy started fiddling with the bent wheel again. "His family sent him to some of them fancy prep schools first. But he never lasted. Had kind of a wild streak to him, I guess."

"You mean they kicked him out?"

Daddy nodded. "Lucky for us they did. Our team was district champions the year he came back. We'd've gone all the way to state if he'd stuck around."

"Where'd he go?"

"Run off and married Clarice Madigan," said Daddy, turning the wheel one last twist. "Prettiest girl in school. Well, next to your mother," he added with a grin, right as Mama walked in the kitchen door.

"You better believe it." She gave him a fake punch in the arm and grinned back.

"You mean he never graduated?" I thought about old high-and-mighty J.D. and all her brain talk. "What was he, dumb or something?"

"Max Monroe? You kidding me? . . . Look there, Maggie, slides as good as new. . . . Naw, Max was smart as they come. Just didn't like school, I guess."

Well, I couldn't fault him there. Plenty times I'd be glad to chuck it myself. But you couldn't just *leave.* . . . "Didn't his folks get mad?"

Daddy looked at Mama with his eyebrows cocked. You know, that way grown-ups do when they ain't sure if the kid asking the question is old enough to hear the answer? I swear, they can drive you nuts with that one. But Mama thought it over some, and then she went ahead and answered me herself.

"Well, naturally they were upset," she said. *"Anybody's* parents would be. We all know there's no substitute for a good education."

I sighed. "Yes, ma'am." Lord, I'd asked a simple question, was all. What did she think I was gonna do, run off and get married next week?

At least Daddy got more to the point. "Rumor was, Mr. Monroe tried to get some judge to break 'em up, but they were both eighteen by then, so there wasn't anything he could do. I guess it made for some pretty hard feelings."

Mama nodded. "They all quit speaking after that. Max didn't even come home for his daddy's funeral."

Good grief. Stuff like that really *happened*? I mean, outside of a television set? No wonder old J.D. was such a nut case. "Well, what's she doing there now, then? The kid, I mean? And the monkey—Mrs. Monroe said her son gave it to her. They friends now, or what?"

This time it was Mama gave Daddy the look. Man, this was getting old. He just looked back at her like, *Your call, ref.* And then she put her hand up to my head and tried to smooth down that cowlick thing. "Jimmy, that little girl's daddy was killed in a car wreck on his way to Houston more than three years ago. I'm sorry, honey, I thought you knew."

CHAPTER fourteen

Aw, man . . .

For a minute I just stood there with my mouth hanging open. Talk about feeling like a jerk. No wonder J.D. had looked at me like that when I asked about her dad being a pro ballplayer. What if she thought I was just fooling with her? That I knew all along and just wanted to make her feel bad?

I wondered what *else* they'd forgot to tell me.

"What about her mom? She ain't dead, is she?"

Mama shook her head. She looked real sorry about the whole thing. "She was driving that day—the little girl was in the car, too. But somehow neither one of them was hurt. Clarice is still over in Houston, as far as I know. I haven't heard a word about her since then. Mrs. Monroe's such a private person; she never discusses her family."

"Then where'd you hear all this?"

"It was in the paper when it happened," said Daddy.

Mama nodded. "We talked about it right here in this

kitchen. I guess I just assumed—but then you weren't but eight years old, were you, Jimmy? No reason you'd remember a thing like that."

Aw, man . . .

My letter to Danny was still sitting in the notebook when I went upstairs. I ripped it out and wadded it up and threw it in the trash with the other one. No way I could quit now. Not with that girl maybe over there thinking I'd been making her the butt of some sick joke. I was just gonna have to go back, that's all, and tell her—

I flopped down on the bed and stared at the ceiling. And tell her *what,* exactly? "Look, I'm sorry about your daddy—I didn't know he was dead, but now I do?" You just can't say a thing like that. I mean, how could you? Ain't polite to point out what a person's got missing.

Aw, man . . .

Next morning me and Mary Al are standing at that gate again like a pair of all-day suckers. You could practically see the cellophane wrapped around us.

"You think she has any *scars* or anything?" Mary Al asked, when I rung the bell. "Maybe that's why she always wears that hat." Her eyes had been about twice their normal size ever since I told her about the accident. Not that I'd wanted to. I just couldn't take a chance on her messing up like me.

"Lord, Mary Al, she don't have scars. We saw her after

she took the hat off, remember? Anyhow, Mama said J.D. didn't get hurt. Just don't *ask* her, for Pete's sake. You got to act regular, you hear me?"

"*I* hear you. You don't have to keep telling me."

"Well, quit looking like that, then."

"Like what?"

"I don't know—you got your face scrooched up all funny."

"I do not."

"You do, too."

"Just shut up about my face, Jim Junior. You ain't the boss of my face. You ain't the boss of the whole dang—"

Skreek! went the intercom. *Skreeeeek!* went the gate.

So we glared at each other real hard and went on in.

It was Mrs. Monroe who opened the front door this time. She looked all puckered up about something. There was some kind of crazy commotion going on behind her—a lot of crashing and hollering and racing around. I looked at Mary Al. She looked at me. *Not again,* we were both thinking.

Crash! Bang! Whomp! "Come here, you stupid—"

"Maybe we've come at a bad time," I started.

"No, no," said Mrs. Monroe, grabbing hold of our hands like she was hanging off a cliff and they was ropes. "Please come in—I have to close this door before—*oh, my . . .*"

We had barely slammed it to when the monkey come flying right at us, screaming and chittering and knocking over a table with a statue sitting on it that was only just the top half of some guy. Mrs. Monroe lunged for it just in the nick and made a diving catch would have done Mike Piazza proud. And then while she's still standing there hugging it like a close friend on the short side, here come J.D. tearing down the big hall and Jasper tearing after J.D., and both of 'em tearing after the monkey, who's bouncing off the walls by now and then leaping onto them crystal lights. And they swing around real pretty and make a nice tinkly sound, but she don't stay there for long. She's heading back up the hallway now, with us five following just as fast as we can.

"Hurry!" cries Mrs. M, "before she goes in the music—oh, no!"

Because sure enough the monkey's high-tailing it in there next and traipsing over the piano keys—*plinkety plunk plink!*—which scares her so bad that now she's *yeeping* worse'n ever and shinnying up that big gold harp. So J.D. makes a grab for her—"Come *here,* you #@*! monkey!"—and it goes crashing over—*kerblam twang twaaannngggg.*

Well, this *really* gets her spooked, so now she's on the run again and knocking over another couple statues—Jasper grabs a half-nekkid lady just in time, but the dude on the horse is a goner—*kersmash!* Then the monkey's out of there—why didn't anybody think to close *that* door? I wonder—but it's too late, she's halfway down the hall again and hitting the library. And by the time the rest of us get there, she's scrambling up the shelves so fast she's knocking down books on our heads—*thwack! ouch! thwack!*—and I only just miss being beaned by *The Call of the Wild.*

"Please!" cried Mrs. Monroe. "Can't someone *do* something?" Meanwhile Jasper was clapping like crazy, but nobody was paying any attention, until I put my little fingers in the corners of my mouth and did my best ear-blasting whistle—

TWEEEEEEEEET!

It worked. It actually worked. I couldn't believe it. I'd been trying to get that right since I was four years old. But for just this once everybody—even the monkey—shut up and stared at me.

"Thank you," I said. "Now, if y'all will just stay real quiet . . . Mary Al, you come on over here and do your crying routine."

"Her *what?*" J.D. began, but Jasper put a finger to his lips, and the rest of us held our breath and watched Mary Al.

"Hello, little monkey," she said, real soft. "You remember me, I know you do. Won't you come down from there and see me, one more time? I'm so sad, little monkey. I'm so saaaad. . . ."

Just like a charm, I swear. Course it took a couple minutes. But Mary Al was a pro, she was wailing up a storm by now. Pretty soon the monkey was pacing around up there next to Plato's *Republic,* looking like she just might bust out crying herself. And in less time than it would take my daddy to sing the first verse of "Heartbreak Hotel," she's down them shelves and safe on Mary Al's shoulder.

"My word," breathed Mrs. Monroe. She was still hanging on to that half of a statue. "I've never seen the like."

"How about that?" I said, all proud. "Nothing to it, if you just know how. Ain't that right, Mary Al?"

But Mary Al looked worried for real. "She's so scared, Jimmy. Her heart's beating way too fast."

"You'd better put her back in her cage," said Mrs. Monroe. "Too much excitement, that's all it is. Jasper, will you take them down?"

Course he nodded and started to show Mary Al the way, and J.D. and me were about to follow, too, but Jasper turned around and shook his head hard and held up his hand to stop us. *No,* he was saying. *Too many people.*

I could see old J.D. balling up them fists again, about to say something we'd all regret, but before she had a chance, Mrs. Monroe stepped in. "I think it would be better if you and James waited in here for a little while, Joy. Just until they get her settled." She put out a hand to check a bump that was coming over J.D.'s left eyebrow where the harp had grazed her. "Are you hurt?" she asked. "Maybe we'd better put some ice on—"

But J.D. jerked away. "It's nothing," she snarled. "What do you care, anyway? All you know how to do is lock things up."

Mrs. Monroe didn't answer right away. Just stood there

facing J.D. with her back so straight you could use it for fence post and that marble man clutched to her chest. I swear, she was getting taller by the second. She waited until Jasper and Mary Al were gone and the sound of their footsteps had died away. Then she turned to me and said, "I'll be in the music room if you need me, James," as if J.D.'s manners were so far below us they'd turned her invisible.

"Yes, ma'am. Could I carry that statue for you?"

"No, thank you. I can manage. But if you could pick up a few of these books, I'd appreciate it."

"Yes, ma'am. We'll get right to 'em."

"Speak for yourself," the wolf girl growled.

But the old lady played like she couldn't *hear* her, either, and she nodded to me and walked out of the room.

CHAPTER fifteen

I didn't say a word. Oh, I *thought* of plenty. But I swallowed 'em whole. You come over here to *apologize,* I told myself. Anything else's gonna just dig you a deeper hole than you got yourself in already.

So I kept my mouth closed and started picking up books, while old J.D. just stood there scowling at me. This went on for eight or nine years, and then—

"So what's wrong with *you?*" she muttered.

I just shrugged and picked up a copy of something so old the pages were all crackly, falling to little brown pieces in my hands. I closed it up and smoothed out its cover. *In Our Convent Days,* I read.

"I asked you a question, James Henry."

"Nothing," I answered. And then I added under my breath, "Ain't nothing wrong with *me.*"

She let this pass. For a minute. And then she started up again. "So why you got that look on your face?"

"What look?"

"*That* look."

I shrugged again, keeping my eyes glued to the paper crumbles I was trying to sweep into the palm of my hand. You ain't the boss of my face, is what I was thinking. But I gritted my teeth, and my lips stayed locked.

This really got her steamed.

"You know what I'm talking about. *That* look right there. Like you think you're so almighty perfect."

"I never said—"

"No, but you're thinking it, aren't you? You think I shouldn't talk to my granny that way, right, James Henry? You think she's such a sweet old lady?"

I didn't look at her. Just climbed this little stepladder that was set up over in the corner and stuck *The Stones of Venice* in a handy gap.

"Old liar, that's what she is," J.D. went on, just as if I'd agreed with her. "Standing there acting like she cares about that monkey. 'Too much excitement'—right, like she really *knows*. She never even looks at it, if she can help it. Keeps it down there in that—that *dungeon*. Never even bothered naming it—how weird is that? Poor thing's been here three years now and still doesn't have a name."

Well, that *was* kind of weird, come to think of it. But maybe there was some mistake. "Maybe you just never heard it, that's all. I bet if you asked her—"

"I did."

"What'd she say?"

"She said I should look under C."

"Under *what?*"

"Under C—for *capuchin*—look, it's right here." J.D. grabbed an encyclopedia off a shelf and flipped through till she had the page. "Capuchin—you got that, James? *Káp-yōo-shin.* One of four species, thought by some to be the most intelligent of all the New World monkeys . . . So called because of a dark patch of hair on the top of the head that resembles a monk's hood, also called a *capuche* . . . Remarkably prolific, highly adaptable, common in Central and South American rain forests from Honduras to Paraguay . . ." She slammed the book shut. "Do you believe that? Real personal, huh? She told me the *kind,* not the name. That'd be like—I don't know—somebody asking me *your* name, and I say, Oh, sure, just look under H for *human.*"

I felt kind of flattered, to tell you the truth. I didn't think she'd noticed. Not that she actually *meant* it or anything. This name deal, though—that couldn't be right. "Well, it's Jasper that takes care of her, and he just can't *say* her name, that's all—"

She gave me one of her squinty-eyed looks. "And we all know why he *can't,* don't we?"

Oh, no, she wasn't gonna get away with that one again. Lucky thing I'd thought to ask about it just this morning. "That's some kind of medical condition, is all. Mama says Jasper had throat cancer awhile back."

J.D. got real quiet. For a few seconds, anyway. I guess the word *cancer* had caught even *her* off guard. But then she shrugged. "Oh, sure, that's what they *say*. What'd you expect, anyway? You think they'd tell your mother anything that mattered?"

I could feel my ears starting to burn, so I gritted my teeth again. Tried counting to ten. She's half an orphan, I told myself. How would you feel in her shoes? No telling what a jerk you'd be. . . . I picked up *The Strange Case of Dr. Jekyll and Mr. Hyde* and shoved it next to *That Hideous Strength*. I wasn't going to say a word. I swear I wasn't.

She stood there watching me for another minute or two. Never lifted a finger while I worked. And then just when I thought I had pretty well talked myself out of choking her—

"It was me that let her out," she said.

Oh, really? *Big* surprise there. *J.D.* let out the monkey! And here all this time I'd been thinking it was *Jasper* got a sudden urge to wreck the joint. I didn't even bother turning my head. "Why would you do a durn fool thing like that?"

"Why do you care?"

"Why do you always say that? Why do I have to care?"

"Why are you always asking stupid questions? Were you dropped on your head, or does it just run in the family?"

Okay, that did it. Dead daddy or no. Wasn't gonna be any apologizing around *here* today. The way I figured it, we were flat-out even.

I turned around and shook my head. "You're sick, you

know that? You're a seriously ill person. But that don't give you any right to talk that way about my family."

But she wasn't looking at me anymore. She was staring out the window.

"Did you hear me?" I asked. "I said it's a shame about your mental problems, but that don't give you the right—"

"I was gonna take her to the island," she said.

"What?" She'd said it so soft I could hardly make it out. "Take who where?"

"The monkey," she said. "That's why I let her out. I wanted to take her to the island."

"Aw, come on. How were you gonna—"

"She'd like it over there—just look at it. All those old twisty trees. The *World Book* says they spend almost all their time in trees. She'd think she was back in the rain forest."

"There are trees around here, too. Jasper takes her out every day."

"Yeah, right—on a *leash*. How'd you like it if the only time you weren't in a cage, you were on some stupid *leash*?"

"Yeah, well . . ." Wasn't any way to answer a question like that. I picked up *Great Expectations*. "How were you planning on getting her there? Freestyle or frog kick?"

J.D. didn't say anything for a minute. Which had to mean trouble. I kept busy with the books, not wanting to pay any mind to someone who didn't deserve it, but I could feel them green eyes burning a hole in my back. Then finally she come up right behind me and growled again, real low, "If I tell you something, you swear to keep your mouth closed?"

"Depends."

"What do you mean, depends? Depends on what?"

"On what you tell me." I climbed back up the ladder. "You tell me you're planning to commit murder, I might have to mention it."

J.D. snorted. "Forget it. I should've known."

"Known what?"

"That you'd be the kind tells 'em every little thing. 'Mama, I'm gonna cross the street.' 'Daddy, it was me broke your pencil.' "

"Now just hold on a—"

" 'Teacher, Billy called me a crybaby three times. . . .' "

"Okay, cut it out. I ain't like that. Nobody tells 'em *everything*."

"You do. Sure you do. A good little boy like Jimmy? You'd have to ask *permission* to go to the island."

"I wouldn't, either. . . . Well, what if I did? Who cares if I ask or not?"

J.D. went into her kindergarten routine again. "Because if the old lady's hiding something over there, she'll just say no, right, Jimbo? And if she's not—well, what's there to ask about? I mean, she never actually said we couldn't go, did she?"

"Well, maybe not, but—"

"But nothing. It's simple. The only reason she might say no is the same reason we can't ask. Don't you see?"

No. I didn't. My head was spinning. Talking to this girl was like trying to get through one of them durn funhouses at the Southeast Texas State Fair—mirrors coming at you every whichaway and shadows messing with your mind and big goofy clown faces popping out when you least expect. All for the solitary purpose of driving you nuts.

Still, one part of what she'd said was true—the old lady had never said we *couldn't* go. Why would she, anyway? Weren't no secrets over there, I'd stake my life on it. So what would be the problem if . . .

I shook myself. What in the world was I thinking? I wasn't actually considering letting this crazy girl talk me *into* something, was I? No way. I guess I had more sense than to—

" 'Mrs. Monroe, can I go to the bathroom now, pleeeeeeeze?' "

"Cut it out, I told you."

"Then swear."

"Swear what?"

"Swear you'll keep your mouth closed if I tell you."

"Tell me *what*?"

"Swear first."

"All right. Fine. You win, okay? I *swear* already." I

climbed back down the ladder and gave it a kick. "So what's your big deal secret, anyhow?"

Miss Joy Monroe smiled and leaned in close. I could all but smell canary on her breath. "I found a boat, James Henry."

CHAPTER sixteen

What she didn't say was *where* she had found it.

"The *graveyard*? Are you kidding me?"

We were standing away over on the far side of the lake, right smack in the middle of all the dead Monroes. Looked like they outnumbered the live ones by a mile. There was Beloved Brothers and Devoted Wives and a whole raft of in-laws and uncles, all tucked up nice and neat in their little stone houses. Every one of 'em sweating less than I was, I guarantee.

I'd followed J.D. over here at a quick trot all the way from the mansion, right after she'd stuck her head in at the music room door. "I'm taking Jim outside to show him around we'll be back when we feel like it see you later," she'd growled at her grandma, spitting it out so fast that all Mrs. Monroe had time to do was look surprised.

"Great, huh?" J.D. said now. "It's the one in back there, off to the side. You can't see it from the big house at all."

"Oh, yeah, great. Are you out of your mind? They keep corpses in them things, not boats!"

"Not in this one, they don't. Come and see."

"Aw, man . . ."

"Don't be scared, little Jimbo." She grinned and pulled me toward it. "I won't let the ghosties grab you."

"Cut it out," I said, jerking my arm away. Was this her idea of a joke? We'd open the durn door and she'd shove me inside and lock it and I'd suffocate and rot and they'd never find me? Now *that* would be a barrel of laughs.

But she didn't, and I didn't, and when she turned the knob and the door creaked open and we pushed aside the cobwebs, the little boat was there, just like she said. Pretty dusty and dirty-looking, but all in one piece, setting up on its end against the far wall. Looked like somebody'd propped it there and left it about a million years ago— along with a pair of old oars and an ancient lawn mower and a rusty rake and a crusted-up hoe and a couple busted hedge clippers and a pair of beat-up garden gloves and half a bag of prehistoric crawfish pellets.

"Well, I'll be dogged," I muttered.

It wasn't a tomb, just a toolshed.

"They must've made it look like the others so it would blend in," said J.D. "Pretty smart, huh? You could put anything you want in here, and nobody'd ever steal your stuff. They'd never even think to look inside one of *these*."

"*You* did."

"Yeah, well, great minds and all that. Come on, let's get this show on the road."

I didn't say anything for a minute, just stood there staring at all the broken-down equipment. They prob'ly had full-time gardeners out here in the old days. Course now we'd see them big crews coming in, two, three times a week. Guys in them outfits bring their own mowers and such, wouldn't have any use for this old stuff. I bet they passed this place a thousand times and never paid it any mind. No real reason they should—

I looked at J.D. "You mean to say you were just strolling along out here yesterday afternoon, and you just *happened* to open this particular door?"

"That's right."

"Well, that was pretty lucky, wasn't it?"

"Yeah, sure, real lucky. Now, come *on,* will you?"

"But how did you know which one to look in? How would you even *think* of looking for a boat in—"

I cut myself short. Man, oh, man. I'd just about gone and done it again, hadn't I? Maybe it wasn't a boat she'd been after at all. That ain't what people go hunting for in their family graveyards.

All of a sudden I got real interested in checking out the hull. "Seems okay," I muttered, wiping off the dust as best I could. "Seems just fine. These aluminum rowboats'll last pretty much forever."

"So you think it'll float?"

I shrugged. "Sure, I guess." I'd been on a thousand

fishing trips with my dad, but he was the real expert. I couldn't very well tell *her* that, though.

"Only one way to find out, right?" said J.D. "Don't just stand there staring. Let's get this thing down to the water."

My stomach gave a sick little lurch. This whole deal was way creepier'n I'd bargained for. "I don't know, J.D. Maybe this ain't such a great idea."

The green eyes slitted up. "Don't chicken out on me now, James Henry. You swore, remember? Or should I go get your little sister, instead?"

Lake Luly was more of a mud color that day, with the sun dipping in and out of clouds. Made it look like the good old swamp it was in its heart. Still had a few of them bald cypress trees standing knee-deep out there, which cheered me up considerable. Probably the whole lake wasn't much over Mary Al's head, I told myself, as we eased the little boat into the water.

Course you couldn't ever tell, was the thing. One minute you're walking along some nice sandy swamp bottom with water just up to your thighs, and then all of a sudden you hit a muddy hole and *kergloop!* You ain't there anymore. But then I was a pretty strong swimmer, and as long as the boat didn't leak, it didn't matter anyway, right?

"You planning on rowing?" I asked, when J.D. plopped herself down by the oars.

"Why not?"

"You know how?"

"What's to know? You stick 'em in the water and shove 'em back and forth, right?"

"Well . . . not exactly. Come on, switch places. I'll teach you, okay? You can try it next trip if this one goes all right."

For once, she didn't argue. Looked like she wanted to, but she didn't. In too much of a hurry to get to the island, I guess. She kind of halfway paid attention to me while I showed her how to work the oars, but all the time she had her eyes fixed on the shore ahead.

"Can't you go any *faster*?" she asked.

"Keep your hat on, will you? We're getting there." I should have said *shirt,* but I was distracted. She had on that crazy wolf hat again, must've pulled it out of her pocket when I wasn't watching. Made her look like some kind of Looney Tune Christopher Columbus.

Course she'd wanted to stop by for the monkey—and Mary Al, too, just to keep the furball calm and all—but I'd said no, not until we'd made sure it was safe. And what would we have told Jasper, anyhow? So finally she'd had to agree it was better this way the first time.

I'd been thinking back there in the graveyard that it might should be the last time, too, but now that we were out on the water it all seemed pretty harmless. It was a tiny bit cooler once we got underway, just a smidgen of a breeze blowing. Little rainbows in the ripples here and there, looking awful pretty. Some kind of oil seeping up from the bottom, I bet. You could put in a well right here, make more money'n you ever dreamed. But then I guess the Monroes had so many oil wells already they were sick of fooling with 'em.

Anyhow, we slipped along real peaceful like this and the island kept getting bigger and bigger, and before we knew it we were sliding onto sand again.

"Now, I call that a perfect landing," I said, jumping out and wading onto the little beach. "Just hop out there and give me a hand, d'you mind? Got to get this boat pulled up here far enough to keep 'er from floating off."

I turned around. J.D. wasn't moving. After all her big-deal hurrying, she was sitting stock-still.

"J.D.?" I said.

Not an eyelash twitched.

"J.D.? You awake? We're here."

CHAPTER seventeen

"J.D.?"

This time she turned her head, at least.

"Can you make it out of there okay?" I asked, offering a hand.

Which she didn't take, of course.

"Yeah, sure," she muttered, coming back to life.

But only a little at a time, in the beginning, almost like she was sleepwalking or something. Didn't say another word—didn't act like she knew I was there, even—only stepped out onto the shore and looked all around, real slow.

It wasn't much different from a hundred swampy islands me and Daddy had fished from or hunted on. All tangly and overgrown, mostly, with them big old strangler vines crawling up into the trees. Sunshine fell through the leaves in little spotty patches, and there was a good lemony smell that had to be magnolia, but I couldn't see where the blossoms were hanging just yet.

A redbird flew right over us, singing, and landed away up high on a sweet gum branch. I think that's about the nicest sound there is. And everywhere around us you could hear that soft little humming that's always in these lonesome places—just a jillion bugs talking and stirring their wings, I guess. Funny thing, though, first thing come to my mind when I heard it this time? How when I was little, I thought it was the way trees purred.

I even almost opened my mouth to say it—J.D. looked like she was listening to it, too. But I couldn't, somehow. She was being so nice and quiet for a change, almost like we were in church. If it weren't for the hat, you might mistake her for a regular kid.

Anyhow, she'd probably just say that was the stupidest thing she ever heard and ruin it.

So I kept quiet, too, and we walked along like that for a while, climbing over fallen logs and staying clear of sticker bushes and keeping an eye out for water moccasins and such, and after a bit we could see the castle towers up ahead.

That was when J.D. started coming awake for real. First she stopped again for a second—so quick I almost run her over—and then she took a deep breath and lit out through the trees.

"Wait up!" I hollered, following as best I could. "You're gonna trip if you ain't careful—"

But she wasn't listening. Not to me. She was gathering speed, if anything, tearing along like her life depended on it. When she come up on a pool-sized puddle, she didn't bother stepping around, just splashed right through and kept on going. Startled doves scattered, gray wings flapping, so close I could feel their wind. A hoot owl opened its eyes and flew away. Lizards scooted under rocks, night frogs started bawling, crows screamed and scolded: *Caw! Caw! Caw!*

And then she was there, she was standing in the castle, and me right behind her, gasping for breath.

"What is it?" I panted. "What are we running for?"

Still she didn't answer. She was looking all around now. Not that there was really a heck of a lot to look at. A plaster shell, is all that castle was, nothing very special up close. Pretty from a distance, but mostly just hollow inside.

"This couldn't be it," I heard her mutter. "I've missed it, somehow. . . ."

"Missed what?" I asked. "What are we looking for, anyway?"

She shrugged and shook her head.

"You mean you don't know?"

"I'll know it when I see it."

"When you *see* it?" I wiped the sweat out of my eyes. "You think that might be sometime this year? It's nearly noon now, no telling where Mary Al thinks I am—"

But she wasn't listening. She was turning around and walking back the way we'd just come. Which at least was in the direction of the boat. So I trotted along beside her without a fight—a little slower this time, thank the Lord.

You could see our two sets of footprints in the muddy places, from us charging along in the opposite direction.

"So I guess it's safe enough," I said after a while, just to be saying something. "I mean, aside from a snake or two. I don't really see anything to worry about, do you?"

No answer.

"I still don't get why it has to be such a big secret, though."

Silence. I might as well been a mosquito buzzing, for all the mind she was paying me.

"Come on, J.D., admit it. Ain't no one hiding anything around here. Only body you're gonna find is mine, when the heat stroke gets me. Next time we got to remember to bring a couple cans of soda pop or—"

"Shh," said J.D., stopping once more. "Do you smell that?"

"Smell what?" I said, sniffing the air. Then I heard how crazy that sounded. "It has to be quiet for you to *smell* something?"

"Shut up," she said. "You know what I mean." She lifted her nose and closed her eyes. I swear, she was up to about 90 percent wolf.

"Can't you smell that?" she asked again. "That lemony smell? That's magnolia, right?"

"Oh, *that*. Sure. I guess it is. I smelled it when we first got here, too."

"I knew it," she said. "I knew I'd missed it. . . ."

I sighed. Here we go again. "Missed *what*?"

But she was already turning away from our fresh-made tracks and forging ahead on a whole new course. Following that flower scent just like a bloodhound. "It's this way, right? Do you still have it, Jim? I'm starting to lose it here. . . . No, there it is again! It must be around here somewhere—"

She broke off all at once.

"J.D.?" I called. I couldn't see her for a minute. "Where are you? You all right?"

I come barreling around a berry bush and almost flattened her again. She was standing still as a statue, looking up. So I followed her eyes, and there it was, the biggest magnolia tree I ever seen. It was loaded with them pretty white blossoms, and bees buzzing around 'em like crazy, and the lemon smell so thick now you could taste it. And setting away up high in its branches was that very same redbird, singing the very same song.

"What?" I said. "It's just a tree, that's all. I mean, it's real nice and everything, but—"

"Shh," she said. "Keep looking."

So I looked some more. . . .

Sure enough, now I could see strips of wood nailed into the trunk like rungs on a ladder, disappearing into the dark green leaves. So then I kept on looking. And after a while I could make out a dilapidated tree house, with a beat-up wooden sign hanging over the door.

"What's it say?" I asked. "Is that a person's name?"

The paint was peeling so bad you could barely make it out.

"No," said J.D. "Look harder."

So I looked one more time, just as hard as I could look, and then I squinted up my eyes and finally I saw.

The sign on the door said ELSEWHERE.

CHAPTER eighteen

"I thought it was only a story," said J.D., so low I almost couldn't hear her. Looked as if she'd weirded out on me again.

"What story?" I asked.

She didn't answer. She was moving toward the magnolia now—but slow, like an underwater swimmer.

I followed her. "What story?"

"Just a story . . ." She had reached the tree now. "A game we used to play. About an empress who lived on a magic island . . ."

I waited for her to go on, but she didn't. She was staring up at that old sign.

"An empress, huh?"

J.D. nodded. "Only nobody knew it. She always wore a disguise."

My eyes went to the wolf hat. "Why'd she want to do that?"

"To fool her enemies," said J.D. "Her magician gave

it to her." She put out a hand and touched the trunk real
easy, the way you do when you're trying to catch soap
bubbles before they bust. "He said as long as she wore it,
she'd be safe."

"Her magician—"

"The Royal Magician of Elsewhere ..." J.D. took
ahold of one of the nailed-on rungs and started climbing.

I kept up as best I could. "Elsewhere? So that was the
name of the island?"

"Because it might be anywhere. Or nowhere. Some
other where, don't you see? No matter how hard you
looked, it was always somewhere else."

"Oh," I said, trying to act more intelligent than I
felt. Didn't seem like the time to tell her how nuts she
sounded.

Turned out she was just getting warmed up. "And it
could change," she said, climbing up another rung. "It was
always changing. Because there weren't any rules, nobody
telling us how it had to be."

"Changing?" I was right behind her. "Changing how?"

"Like, if it was August, and I wanted snow—if the
Empress wanted snow, I mean—then the Royal Magician
would make me a blizzard. Or if I said, no, roller coasters,
we'd have a whole carnival. Or say I felt like seeing the
year 3000, or the day Noah loaded the Ark. You just name
it—*poof!* There it was. Or sometimes—"

"Watch out!"

One of them old wood pieces had pulled loose under

her foot and come tumbling down, barely missing my head. "You okay?" I called, bracing myself to catch her.

But J.D. had already swung herself up the rest of the way and was sitting inside the tilted one-hinge door. "Or sometimes," she went on, as I clambered up behind her, "sometimes I'd just want to hang around my magic tower."

I looked at the mildewed board I was perched on. "Your magic tower?"

She nodded.

"And *poof*—there it was?"

"There it was. . . ."

We were both quiet for a minute then. Just sat there looking around us. Lord, what a mess. Maybe the old place had been all right once upon a time, but now it was more tree than house. Them big white flowers poking in through every gap they could find. And there was plenty to find, I'm here to tell you. Giant gashes in what was left of the roof and rusty nails sticking out where the floorboards had rotted through and at least two moldy bird's nests hanging out of what used to be a window.

"You sure this is it?" I asked, after a while. "I mean, that castle wasn't all that bad."

"Yes, it was. It was a gyp, you saw it. Just one of those big empty shell things they think we like."

I looked through the hole in the roof to the clouded-up sky. "But at least it would keep the rain off," I said. "And it has towers, too—"

She shook her head. "Not like this one." She studied

a bruised white petal that had fallen into her lap. "He said he built it with magic wood, disguised as a magnolia tree."

"The magician?" I asked.

"The magician," she answered.

I lifted a corroded piece of two-by-four that turned to mush in my hand. "Well, if this is his idea of magic wood," I began—*I wouldn't want him sawing me in half,* I was about to say.

But then I saw her face, and I shut my mouth. Good Lord. She was talking about her daddy, wasn't she? Well, sure she was. Who else would've built this old tree house and told her all them stories? And I was just now *getting* it? Good Lord.

I expected she'd take my head off again. Or at least push me out of the tree. Might've even made me feel a little better, as a matter of fact.

But she didn't do either one. Just sat there awhile more, real quiet. And then she said, "I always thought it was only in our heads. That he'd made it all up out of nothing, just for me." She ran her finger along a big crack in the floor, like she'd never seen anything so amazing. "But it was here, don't you get it?" She looked up, with them green eyes shining. "It was here all along. And I never knew."

"Until you found the boat?"

She grinned. "Even that was part of it. In the story, I mean. The secret barge to Elsewhere. He always said it was buried in a tomb."

"Or what *looked* like a tomb—"

"Exactly."

"Jeez Louise . . ." I shook my head. I swear, it was just like *Treasure Island* or something. Well, except we had a monkey, not a parrot. And I guess there wasn't much use in us digging for a chest of gold. And Jasper wasn't exactly my idea of Long John Silver. . . .

"So how long you think it'll take us to fix it up?"

"What?" I'd kind of lost track there for a minute.

"The tree house, dummy."

I stared at her. "*This* tree house?"

"How many tree houses you been in today?"

"Aw, man, J.D.—" I shook my head. "You have any idea how hard that would be? I mean—how could we? Where would we get the wood? How would we get it *over* here? It'd be one thing if the bridge was still there, but in that little boat? There's no way, that's all. It's the craziest thing I ever—I mean, how *could* we?"

She sat there real serious, nodding and listening, until I finally ran out of breath. And then she leaned in close and clapped her hand on my shoulder. "You'll think of something."

I groaned. *"J.D.—"*

But she was already climbing down them rickety rungs. "Come on, Jimbo, don't just sit there. I'm starving. Watch out for that next-to-last one. It's a doozy. . . ."

CHAPTER nineteen

I worried the whole way back to the big house about leaving Mary Al on her own all this time. But when we finally got there, we found her setting up real prim and prissified at that mile-long dining room table, having lunch with Mrs. Monroe and our mother. I'd forgot it was Mama's day to do the old lady's hair—looked like she'd shampooed, cut, set, blow-dried, curled, and combed, all while we were out there sweating on the island.

"There they are!" Mary Al hollered, dropping her fork and her manners both at once. There was a little green piece of a lettuce leaf hanging out the corner of her mouth.

Mrs. M didn't seem to notice, though. She looked— well, kind of hopeful, somehow. "Did you have a nice walk? Do sit down, you must be hungry. . . . We were sorry to start without you, but we just weren't sure. . . ."

"Who's *she*?" J.D. growled. I'd already slid into a chair, hoping nobody would notice my muddy shoes, but J.D.—

who'd been almost *normal* for the last hour—just slouched there under that wolf hat, scowling at my mother.

"Oh, I'm sorry," said her grandma. "I forgot you two hadn't been introduced. Maggie, this is my granddaughter, Joy Monroe. Joy, this is your friends' mother, Mrs. Harbert."

"Hello," said Mama, standing right up and holding out her hand. "I'm so glad to meet you, Joy."

"J.D.," muttered J.D., balling up her fists and burying 'em in her folded-up arms.

Mama nodded and lifted her hand to straighten an earring, just as if that was what she'd meant to do all along. "Well, all right, then, honey. J.D. it is. What does the D stand for?"

"Delinq—" Mary Al started to answer, but I got in a kick under the table just in time.

"Dolores," said Mrs. Monroe.

Dolores? I looked at J.D., who shot me a narrow green glare: *You ever say a word about it you're dead meat, buddy.*

Course Mama missed all that. "Joy Dolores," she was saying now, all friendly and innocent. "What a pretty name. Real musical-sounding . . ."

"*J.D.,*" snarled J.D. "You deaf, or what?" And she turned her back to us and stomped out.

We all just sat there staring at our spoons, and then Mama looked at Mrs. Monroe. "I'm sorry," she said. "I didn't mean—"

"No, no, please," said Mrs. Monroe. "*I'm* sorry." She'd

gone all stiff again. "I can't imagine what you must . . .
Of course, there's no justifying . . ."

From down the hall we could hear the sound of a door
being slammed.

Mrs. Monroe cleared her throat. "You'll excuse me,
won't you?" And she stood up and left the room.

Whatever it was she'd been hoping for, it was over now.

Daddy was sitting at the kitchen table when we got home,
taking his new aptitude test. He'd called up a number
they advertised on TV and ordered it from the Lone Star
Academy of Court Reporting. He was only on page two,
but he looked pretty sick of it already, trying to rub out a
pencil mark in one of them little circles.

You never saw anybody seem gladder to be interrupted.
"So," he said, getting up and stretching, "how'd it go
today?"

"Great," said Mary Al. "I got to feed the monkey and
hold her and walk her around and then Mama come and
we ate little bitty sandwiches and J.D. was rude and we
had fruit salad and I finished it all but the mushmelon."

Daddy shook his head. "Sounds like quite a morning.
And what about you, son? Any better today?"

I didn't really know how to answer that. "I guess it
could've been worse," I said finally. "At least she didn't
bite us. And we got paid," I added, pulling nine brand-
new dollar bills out of my pocket to show him. "I figure

if I can last six weeks, I might can save up enough to go to Phoenix."

"Oh, I almost forgot," said Mama. "Danny's mother called right after you left this morning. She wanted to give us their new address and phone number."

"She did?" I jumped right out of the chair I had just sat in. "Why didn't you tell me? Where'd you write it down? Can I call him now?"

"No, honey, he won't be there now—not until after the weekend. Janie said he'd just left on a camping trip."

"A camping trip?" But he just *got* there. "Did he go with his dad, or what?"

"I don't think so, Jimmy. I believe she said it was a new neighbor who'd invited him."

A new neighbor? Some kid, then? Danny'd been gone three days and he'd already made a new friend?

I guess Mama saw the look on my face, because she added in a hurry, "But you had another call right after that—Conrad Smith's mother invited you and Mary Al to go bowling with their family this evening. Won't that be fun?"

Oh, brother. Not Conrad Smith. "You didn't say I'd *go,* did you?"

But she had, of course, since Conrad's sister Cecilia was just Mary Al's age, and she was sure I'd enjoy it, too, and Mr. and Mrs. Smith were just *such* nice people. . . .

So because my mother was so worried about the sorry state of my social life, I spent the best hours of a Friday night trapped in a bowling alley with the biggest, braggingest blowhard in the tricounty area. Listening to him tell me how his Uncle Fritz had bowled a perfect game three times and taught him a foolproof way to knock down the seven-ten split and he wished he could tell me but it was a family secret and by the way (he whispered while his mother was wading down the gutter to where Cecilia's ball was stuck still as a pumpkin) did I want to go spying with him later because he had a new set of binoculars cost forty-nine ninety-nine and he knew of this teenage girl's house with a backyard pool and she looked like the type who might swim nekkid.

Man, what a jerk.

> *"Dear Danny,"* I wrote in the notebook when I got home, *"I was going to call you today but your mom said you'd gone camping with your new friend. Where'd you go, the Grand Canyon or something? I guess y'all are having a real good time—"*

I put down my pen. Didn't feel much like writing. Bowling with Conrad had pretty much done me in. To tell you the truth, I'd rather put up with the wolf girl than a guy like that. All sweet as pie when the grown-ups were around. Old J.D. might be meaner'n sin, but at least she wasn't sneaky about it. She treated everybody the same way—bad.

I climbed into bed and turned out the light. Course she was crazy as they come. Talking about how we could fix up that old tree house. *You'll think of something.* . . . She had no idea how hard that would be. She might be smart about some things, but she didn't have clue one about carpentry. Why, if she was doing it by herself, she'd get it all wrong. Prob'ly mess it up worse'n it already was. No telling what would happen. She wouldn't know how to look for the rotten places. Might just fall through and break her fool neck.

I doubt she even knew what a plumb bob was.

The moonlight was shining on my bulletin board. I stared at it for a while. Had that picture of Danny and me tacked up on it, from the fair last year. Danny had on a Bozo-the-Clown nose and some of them plastic vampire fangs, and he was smiling real goofy and making devil fingers over my head. That was a great day. I remember right when Mama took the snapshot. It was just before we rode the Bullet and I threw up and we had to go home.

Weird thing, though. Here Danny had been gone just three days and I couldn't quite picture his face—any other way than it was in the photo, I mean. I closed my eyes and tried as hard as I could, but the big nose and teeth were still there. It really bothered me, you know? Three days and three nights and already he was getting hazy.

No wonder he'd gone camping with his new neighbor. Somebody with a better head for faces than me, I bet.

Somebody who could at least remember what his best friend *looked* like. . . .

I turned over and stared out the window at the ghost lights. I wondered could J.D. remember her daddy's face. Three *years* he'd been gone, and a heck of a lot further than Phoenix.

Well, shoot. There *was* that old pile of lumber Uncle Will left in the carport when he tore down his duck blind last fall. Mama'd be glad to be rid of that. And maybe there was something we could salvage from out of that toolshed tomb. And maybe if we didn't try to load up the boat too much on each trip and if we worked on it every day after we fed the monkey and maybe picked up just one or two things down at the hardware store . . .

I looked at the nine dollars folded up on my dresser. It was way more than I thought I'd earn this soon. Maybe I could use just a *couple* bucks to get us started.

I closed my eyes and took a deep breath and let it out real slow. I'd have to run by Handy Dan first thing in the morning. Even on a magic island, when there's hammering ahead, you best be sure you got the nails.

CHAPTER twenty

Next couple weeks slid by slick as goose grease. And this right after the *slowest* three days ever was. I never could understand how time works so crazy that way—always speeding up and slowing down, like a busted clock. Course Mama says it flies when you're having fun, but I ain't sure you'd call it that. We were mostly just hammering and sweating. Still, I didn't mind it too much, and at least nothing really *bad* happened. Fact is, for the next two weeks we didn't run up against a single problem wouldn't all but volunteer to solve itself.

Problem number one: lumber. Nothing to it, after all. Uncle Will's old two-by-fours turned out to be just the ticket. And I was right about Mama, too—she was so pleased to get that mess cleared, she was practically tap dancing in the carport. Claimed she'd been thinking about having herself a bonfire come fall, anyway.

Course Daddy did wonder what I was needing all that wood for. And I didn't want to lie to him, but J.D. had sworn me not to tell, so I ended up saying it was kind of a secret project.

"Oh," he said, grinning a little. "Gonna build you a hideout, huh?"

I guess I turned pretty red.

"Aw, that's all right, son. I'm just teasing you, is all. I know you wouldn't ask if it wasn't okay." He chuckled a little. "Me and Will and Charlie Houston and his cousin Jack Hunter had us a great secret hideout when we were about your age. Least, we thought it was secret. I remember one time we were trying to sleep out there, when old David Rogers come sneaking up on us, started howling just like a coyote. Like to scared us all to death. You never heard such hollering. And then another time—"

He stopped there.

"Another time what?"

But he just chuckled again and shook his head. "Oh, nothing you need to hear." He gave me a look. "You kids plan on behaving yourselves, I hope."

"Yessir."

"Well, all right then. Long as you're not damaging any property or anything."

"Oh, no sir." Now, that was the gospel truth. "We're fixing it up, is what we're doing."

And that was pretty much all there was to problem number one.

Course we still had to worry about number two: getting the lumber to the island. But even that wasn't anywhere near as hard as I thought. Just took a little planning and some muscle. Every morning when we went to work at the mansion, me and Mary Al would haul as many boards as we could manage over to the big gate, then leave 'em propped up behind the azalea bushes once we got inside. Then after we'd get done feeding the monkey and walking her around and all that, we'd put her back in the cage and go on outside again and pick up our lumber and whatever other supplies we'd brought and carry 'em over to that old toolshed. And then we'd stash whatever extra we had in there and haul the rest out with the boat, then load 'er up and head over to the island.

It was a good bit of work—I'm not claiming it wasn't—but nothing we couldn't handle. Even if I did spend half the time looking over my shoulder. Meanwhile old J.D. pitched right in, I'll say that for her, and Mary Al almost always did her part.

Which brings us to problem number three: getting Mary Al to keep quiet. Course I figured that would be durn near impossible. But you know, she was real good about it once she understood it was supposed to be a secret. Never said a single word. Though to tell you the truth, I wouldn't really have minded if she had. I just couldn't see why we had to be so all-fired closemouthed about it. I mean, it wasn't as if we were doing anything *wrong*. Still, I couldn't throw off the feeling that it wasn't quite right, either, sneaking around like this behind the old lady's back. She was my *boss,* for crying out loud.

But J.D. just about snapped my head off when I brought it up one time while we were loading the boat. *"No!"* She spun around and glared at me. "You tell her and I'll—"

"You'll what?" I looked at her balled-up fist. The scab on her knuckles was only now starting to heal. "What's the big deal, J.D.?"

She didn't answer right away. Just dropped the fist and folded up her arms and stared out at the island for a minute. "It would ruin everything," she said finally. "It wouldn't be ours anymore. It wouldn't be Elsewhere, don't you get it?"

I wasn't sure I did. But the way she looked when she said it—well, I kept my mouth closed after that. I'd just never seen a person *want* anything so hard.

Anyhow, I figured, we weren't hurting anybody. It was only a game, that's all. It was even kind of fun when I thought about it that way—like we were spies on a secret mission behind enemy lines. Mary Al was just crazy for the whole idea.

"Red alert! Red alert!" she'd holler about every five minutes, while me and J.D. were hammering on the tree house. She was supposed to be our lookout, you see, even though there never was much to look out for but birds and bugs and lizards and one lunatic squirrel that must've got stranded here when they tore down the bridge.

"Is it Thursday again?" J.D. hollered back this one

morning. Not that she was wanting to know the day of the week. Thursday was what she'd named the squirrel, was all, sort of after that guy Friday in *Robinson Crusoe*.

"It's him, all right," Mary Al yelled. "Got that same little torn place in his tail. And he's acting real goofy, like he done before."

"What's he doing this time?"

"He's chasing himself around a tree."

"He's what?"

"Chasing himself around a tree. His tail keeps curving around it, so he thinks it's another squirrel."

"Poor old Thursday," said J.D. She was tapping the finishing nails in the floorboards the way I'd showed her, while I tore out the new hinge I was trying to fit on the door for the umpteenth time. "I guess he's lonesome."

I looked at her sideways, sitting there in her wolf hat, pounding away with that little ball peen hammer I'd bought. It just wasn't the kind of thing I expected coming out of her mouth. But then she wasn't her usual snarly self over here on the island. It quieted her down, some way. Almost had me halfway believing in magic spells.

Course quick as we'd set foot back in the big house, she'd turn toad again. I swear, you could set your watch by her. Growling at her grandma for no good reason and hissing at me if I looked at her crooked. After that she'd usually go slamming up to her room, and Mrs. Monroe would get real quiet and straight-backed, and then she'd thank us and pay us, and me and Mary Al would go home.

But it wasn't just the money made me bite my tongue every time I felt like saying "I quit." I'da been long gone if it wasn't for this island person.

"Throw Thursday a couple more of them Fritos, Mary Al," I called down now. "That'll settle him some. Gonna give himself a heart attack if he ain't careful."

"What he needs is company," said J.D. She was sucking on a nail. "How soon you think we can bring the monkey over?"

"I don't know. Pretty soon, I guess. Don't swallow that thing, J.D."

She took the nail out of her mouth and tapped it in the wood nice and straight. "How 'bout tomorrow, then?"

Well, shoot. Personally I wasn't all that anxious to find out if monkeys liked boats, but it looked like J.D. wasn't gonna let go of this one, no matter what. She'd been keen to get the furball over here from the start, of course, but up till now there hadn't been any way to do it. Jasper was always there, was the trouble—never mind what Mrs. Monroe had said about us freeing him up for his other duties. He kept an eagle eye on us the whole time we tended that monkey.

Especially on J.D. He didn't trust her for a second. But lately she hadn't given him any reason to complain, just watched from a distance, mostly, even though you could tell she was itching to get closer.

And then just yesterday morning—two weeks to the day after we started the job—Jasper had showed the three

of us to the cellar door and handed me the key. *This is it,*
he was saying. *Graduation day. You're on your own, amigos.*
And then he'd walked away and left us standing there
staring at one another.

"Now," J.D. had whispered, all excited. "We can take
her to the island now."

"Not yet," I'd argued. "We have to make sure she's
ready. She might get nervous when Jasper's not around."

But she'd been just fine, was the thing. Not a trouble
in the world. . . .

The hammer came down again—*bam! bam! bam!*

"Tomorrow," said J.D.

"Tomorrow," I sighed.

Looked like problem number four was floating dead
ahead.

CHAPTER twenty-one

"Come on, Jimmy, what's taking you so long?" Mary Al complained, while I finished my second bowl of Raisin Bran. I didn't usually eat that much, but I had a feeling I was gonna need my strength today.

"Hold your horses, Mary Al," I grumbled. "Not like there's a fire or anything. We ain't but five minutes late."

Daddy lowered his newspaper an inch and looked at me over the top of the want ads. "You feeling all right, son?"

"Yessir, I'm all right."

"Well, you best get moving then. Five minutes late for work is five too many."

"Yessir."

I took one last bite of cereal and sat there chewing and stewing. Wished I could go on back to bed, is what I wished. The more I thought about all the things that could go wrong with that squirmy little monkey in a rowboat, the grouchier I got. Why'd I ever say yes to a durn fool thing like that? I swear, that girl didn't have the sense she was born with, and here I was dancing to her tune like some kind of show dog every time I turned around. Well, it was time to put my foot down, that's all. Just go over there and explain that I'd changed my mind. It was a dumb idea, and dangerous to boot—the island was fine and the monkey was fine but not the two together. And if J.D. didn't like it, well, she could just—

"*Jimmy!* You coming or not?"

I pushed my chair back. It made a nice loud satisfying scraping sound that did me no end of good. "I'm coming," I muttered. "You happy?"

It was Jasper who opened the front door for us, which surprised me some. As fired up as J.D. had acted about the monkey's first boat trip, I figured she'd be pacing the porch with bells on, wondering where we were. But there wasn't any sign of her.

"Is J.D. already down in the storage room?" I asked.

Jasper shook his head and pointed upstairs.

Which I took as a hopeful sign. "Well, maybe she's catching cold or something. I guess we shouldn't bother her to—"

Jasper held up his hand to stop me. *Upstairs,* he pointed again. Though why in the world he cared whether or not J.D. helped us feed the monkey, I couldn't have told you.

"Okay," I sighed. "We'll get her."

Jasper seemed to think we knew where we were going now, so he left us to fend for ourselves. We climbed them twisty stairs again and wandered around some till we found what looked like the hall we'd gone down that first time. But there were so many doors, all closed just like before, I wasn't quite sure I remembered which one it was. Seemed to me it was on the left up there a bit, about halfway down the—

"Did you hear that?"

The creak of a floorboard and a shadow of a movement out the corner of my right eye had made me turn my head in that direction. All the doors weren't closed, after all. Here was one that was partly open, and when I looked inside, I could see J.D. standing in there with her back to us. She was wearing a coat, for some reason—somebody's old overcoat that was way too big for her—and staring at her reflection in a dresser mirror.

"J.D.?"

She jumped and turned around real quick, glaring already. "You ever hear of knocking?"

"Sorry," I said. "The door was open."

"Well, *close* it then," she hissed. "Don't just stand there looking stupid."

Mary Al stuck her chin out. "Don't call Jimmy stupid—"

"I'll call him anything I—"

"Who opened that door?" said an icy voice.

I swung around now and found Mrs. Monroe standing just behind me in the hall, looking, well, *pleased* ain't the word, that's for sure.

"It was open when we got here," I tried to explain, but she wasn't listening to me, she was pushing past me and Mary Al and walking inside and then stopping—dead still—when she saw J.D. in that coat.

I heard of people saying somebody looked like they seen a ghost, and now I knew what they meant. It was like she couldn't breathe right for a minute. There was muscles working funny in her jaw—like she *wanted* to say something, but couldn't do that, either. Meanwhile J.D. just stood there staring her full in the face, with *her* jaw jutted out, too, so for the first time it struck me there wasn't any denying they were kin.

Nobody said a word for what seemed like eight or nine years, so while we were all just standing there like a bunch of waxworks in a sideshow, I looked around a little. It was a boy's room we were in, a teenage boy's who'd played sports. There was a bunch of old trophies, for baseball mostly, sitting on the dresser, and a couple bats and a glove propped up in a corner and a guitar with broken strings sticking out of it and Led Zeppelin and Pink Floyd posters on the wall and an old stereo with record albums lined up in the case under it and one of them radio-controlled cars on the bedside table and a baseball cap that said Calder Wildcats hanging on one of the bedposts. And except that all the stuff looked to be from about twenty years ago, you'd think that the kid still lived here—that maybe he'd just stepped out for a minute before his mama yelled at him to pick up his mess. The bed looked kind of rumpled, and there was a shirt tossed on it, and a stray sock lying on the floor, and a couple beat-up notebooks with cartoons scribbled on the covers and trash still half filling the wire basket on the side of the desk. . . .

"Take off the coat," said Mrs. Monroe. She didn't yell or anything—her voice was real low and quiet, and kind of hoarse-sounding, like maybe she had a sore throat. But there was something terrible in the way she said it, something that raised the gooseflesh clear up to my ears.

J.D. must have felt it, too. She didn't fight back or growl some insult like I was expecting. She just held real still for a few more seconds. Then she took off the coat and threw it on the floor, as if she never cared about it anyway. And then she brushed past us into the hall and went running down to her own room and went inside and slammed the door.

Me and Mary Al didn't move a muscle. I didn't have any idea what to do. I thought sure Mrs. Monroe would turn around and look at us and say something, anything, but she didn't even seem to know we were there. She stayed frozen, same as us, for another minute. And then she walked over to where J.D. had dropped the coat and picked it up and just stood there holding it.

I hope I never see a face so sad again.

Mary Al was looking at me, like *What do we do now?*

But I still didn't know. It didn't seem polite to say anything, but walking out didn't seem exactly right, either, so finally I just cleared my throat real soft.

Mrs. Monroe kind of came to, then. She only glanced our way, was all, but at least that was something. Then she carried the coat to the closet and started hanging it up.

"We'll—we'll be tending to the monkey now, Mrs. Monroe," I said to her back.

She nodded a little. "Fine," she murmured.

And then I grabbed ahold of Mary Al and pulled her along with me and got out of there just as fast as I could.

I didn't much want to knock on J.D.'s door, but I figured I'd better, so I did. Not real hard, only a couple little taps, was all. There wasn't any answer, so I knocked once more, just a tiny bit louder—

"Maybe she don't feel like coming today," said Mary Al.

"I guess not." It was a relief, to tell you the truth. Wouldn't have been any picnic with her in this mood. I turned around. "Well, we tried, anyway—"

The door banged open behind me.

I sighed and swung around again, expecting a whole string of cuss words. But at first J.D. didn't say anything, just stood there glaring at us with her mouth shut tight and her breathing all screwed up.

"What do *you* want?" she finally muttered.

My mind was a blank. What *did* I want?

I wanted to go home. I wanted to get out of this sad old house that made everybody hurt so bad. Most of all I wanted her to quit looking at me that way—like some little kid on the playground who keeps getting knocked down hard and tries to pretend he don't care even if it's killing him.

But I didn't say any of that. How could I? And I didn't give the big speech I'd been planning at breakfast. I cleared my throat and I opened my mouth and I heard myself say, "If we're taking the monkey to the island, we'd better get started."

CHAPTER twenty-two

Turned out I'd been worrying for nothing. That little furball acted like she'd been riding in boats all her life. Just sat there real snug and happy in Mary Al's lap, eating grapes and chittering away, while Mary Al kept up a soft kind of pattering talk:

"You see, little monkey, it's a real nice boat, ain't it? And you're being such a good girl, too. If you keep being good maybe we'll be able to take off that leash pretty soon. . . ."

"We ought to call her something besides little monkey," I said, just to be saying something. J.D. hadn't said a word the whole trip, so far. She'd left off the wolf hat, so as not to scare the monkey, but even without it she was looking fairly lethal. She was sitting there like a coiled steel trap, just waiting for somebody to set her off.

I hoped it wasn't gonna be anybody I knew.

"So what do you think, J.D.?" I asked, hoping to get her smoothed out a little. "You were the one talking about how weird it is, her not having a real name."

She just shrugged.

"How about Goldie? She's got them nice goldy colors all mixed up in her fur, and in her eyes, too, see there?"

No answer.

"You don't like Goldie? Well, maybe something starting with M, so it kind of goes together. You know— Mandy the Monkey or Myrtle or Mildred or Minnie— sure, Minnie the Monkey! What do you think of that?"

J.D. rolled her eyes.

"That sounds too much like Minnie Mouse," said Mary Al.

"Oh, yeah. I guess it does. Well, what about Maureen? That's a real nice name."

"Or Maggie," Mary Al suggested.

"You can't name a monkey after our *mother*—"

"Why not?"

"You just can't, that's all. . . . I got it—Millicent! Remember, Mary Al, old Millicent Phipps used to baby sit us sometimes when you were little?"

Mary Al shook her head.

"Oh, sure you do. You were crazy about her. But then Mama had to let her go. . . ."

"Why?"

"Because she picked her teeth and carried a pistol in her purse and voted for herself in the last election."

J.D. snorted a little at that. "She did not, either," she muttered.

"Yes, ma'am, I swear. Old Millicent was a humdinger,

I'm here to tell you. Oh, yeah, I believe that's the one, all right. Millicent—I like the sound of that, don't you? Millicent Monroe the Magnificent Monkey. Look how she likes it already!"

The monkey just blinked her big eyes real solemn and skinned another grape with them sharp little teeth. She tried to put it in Mary Al's mouth, but even Mary Al had her limits. She made a face and said, "*Eeyyooo*, no, thank you."

Well, anyway, I jabbered on real foolish like that for the rest of the trip. I don't know that it really helped all that much—I mean, J.D. never out-and-out *smiled*—but at least she wasn't looking quite so hair-triggered by the time we slid onto the little beach.

"Can we take off the leash now, Jimmy?" Mary Al asked, as soon as we all climbed out.

"No," I said. I had to draw the line somewhere. "What if she runs away?"

"She ain't gonna run away. It's just a little island— how far could she get? Anyhow, she's being real good today. Just look at her."

It was true. I swear, it was almost as if she knew something special was happening. She got near as quiet as J.D. had done our first time here. Even when Mary Al put her down, she just stood there, staring, like she was remembering something. I wondered, did it look like home?

She glanced back at us after a minute or so—just making

sure we were all still there, I guess. And then she turned around again and took a couple baby steps toward the trees. . . .

And just when I was thinking, well, maybe we could take the leash off for just a *little* while and see how it goes—

There was this loud *click click clicking* noise, and the leaves went to shivering and shaking, and that lunatic squirrel come charging out of the bushes.

"Yeep!" yelled the monkey, scared out of her wits and jumping up so fast that she pulled the leash right out of Mary Al's hand.

"Get her!" I yelled, but it was too late, she was already heading into all them tangly vines and twisty old live oaks, and Thursday was chasing right after her. And then they were both screaming and screeching and tearing through the treetops, and we all tried to keep up, but of course we couldn't, and we couldn't see anything, either, except branches trembling and spooked birds flying every whichaway and maybe just a little streak of fur now and again, but it was pretty hard to tell who it belonged to, and Mary Al was hollering, "Little monkey! Come back!" and J.D. was cussing, and I was seriously considering taking up the habit myself—

When all of a sudden J.D. put up her hands and looked at us and said, *"Shh!"*

So we all hushed up, and sure enough all the other noises had stopped, too—no yeeping or chittering or clicking or any of that. The whole island was quiet, like it was listening, too—not a sound but the little waves lapping and them purring trees.

"Oh, Lord," I muttered. "He's killed her, ain't he? That maniac squirrel has killed the monkey. I knew we shouldn't have ever brought her over—"

"Shh," J.D. said again, shooting green-eyed bullets my way. So I shut up one more time, while she made little pointing signs to the three of us: *I'll go this way,* she was saying, *and you go there, and Mary Al goes there. . . .*

Mary Al nodded in her best spy mode and crept away, and I sighed and headed in the other direction. It was useless, was what it was. He'd killed her, I felt it in my bones. And now we'd have to find her poor little body and bury it. And even if he hadn't killed her, how would we ever know? Even on an island small as this one, there must be a million places they might hide.

Well, shoot. We'd have to go back, that's all, and try to explain the whole thing to Mrs. Monroe—and to Jasper, too, which would be even worse. No telling what he'd do if—

"Oof!"

I had rounded that same berry bush and run smack into Mary Al. J.D. was beside her, standing right where she'd been when we first seen the giant magnolia. They were both staring up into its branches.

"What's going—"

"Shh," said J.D. She pointed to the tree house.

We'd done a pretty good job on it, if I do say so myself. It was a far cry from the rickety mess we'd found just two weeks ago. Wooden rungs all shored up good and strong and mostly sturdy walls and a nice flat floor, though you couldn't really see that from here. Course the roof could still use a bit of work—I was thinking about putting a tarp over it later—but even that had most of the worst gaps filled in.

The Elsewhere sign was painted up nice and fresh, too—that green and gold acrylic paint had set me back ten bucks, but it was worth it. You could see it catching the sunlight, even from here. . . .

And right under it there, where the front door had swung open a little—I still hadn't got them durn hinges straight—the monkey was sitting up calm as you please, chewing on a magnolia blossom.

"Well, I'll be," I breathed.

J.D. looked at me and smiled.

"We'll call her the Empress," she whispered.

CHAPTER twenty-three

Dear Danny,

I been meaning to write you a while now, how's everything in ~~Phe~~ Arizona? I got a job over at the Monroe place right after you left and I been saving my money for more than a month so I could come see you. I thought I'd have plenty by now but keeping ahold of it is harder than I thought. But anyway my Aunt Betsy works at Travel Unlimited and Daddy says I might have enough for one of them cheap fares pretty soon if I can avoid any further ~~expindechurs expendatoors~~ payouts. So I was thinking maybe next month before school starts if it's okay with you, I mean with your folks and all and if you're not too busy or anything.

Sincerely yours,
Your best friend from Texas,
James Henry Harbert, Jr.

I put down my pen and looked over what I'd written and felt pretty good about it up to a point. There was a whole lot more I could have said, but it was too much to fit in an envelope and some of it was supposed to be secret and just thinking about it made my hand cramp up.

Course it would be a lot easier telling it all in person or even on the phone, but it seemed like every time I tried to call him, Danny was out somewhere. Not that I blamed him or anything—I mean, I wouldn't want him to be sitting home bored.

Anyhow, I'd been pretty busy myself.

We'd settled into a fairly good routine with the Empress and the island. She'd got to where she knew that's where we were going just as soon as we'd come down the stairs every morning. You never saw anybody look so happy. It's hard to describe how a monkey looks happy, but there ain't no doubt about it when they do. They start that little chittering sound and their eyes get all sparkly, and when you hold 'em you can feel their hearts pounding—but not like they're afraid. You can tell the difference every time, I swear.

Take the Empress. Every now and then she still got kind of nervous about that maniac squirrel, but she was smarter than he was, by a mile. Within a week she'd figured out that when he made his daily kamikaze attacks he was only bluffing and probably a whole lot more scared of her than she was of him. So in the mornings when we got to the island—we always took off the leash now as soon as we landed—she'd just go on about her regular routine, climbing around in the trees and checking out the territory and eating whatever flowers or berries or bugs she might find. Sometimes she'd eat a lizard or a frog, maybe, which grossed Mary Al out considerable. But then I explained about the law of the jungle and how even a monkey needs protein, and she still didn't like it much, but after a while she got used to it.

So anyhow, the Empress was happy as could be, just minding her own business. And then somewhere usually about half past ten, old Thursday would come charging out of the trees, clicking and chattering and twitching that poor beat-up tail for all it was worth. But the Empress knew how to handle him now. She'd either just hop in through the tree house window and hang out with us for a while, or she'd scramble up a live oak and throw a few nuts at him, which scared him so bad he'd never try to follow. Though we did catch him burying some of 'em later, like that had been his plan all along.

I'da almost felt sorry for the poor fool, if he hadn't started stealing our stuff.

"Mary Al? Did you take my paint rag?"

"What paint rag?"

"My paint rag—the one I always use. I left it right here."

"What would I want with your old paint rag?"

"Well, I don't know. You didn't see it, did you, J.D.?"

"No, but have you seen those two pink candles I brought over? Or the rule book from the Monopoly game?"

"Not lately—"

"Well, where could they have gone? We never took 'em out of here. . . ."

We couldn't figure it out at first, but then we started seeing the evidence scattered under the trees. Little scraps of ragged cloth with paint stains on 'em and shredded bits of paper with half-words like "mmunity Chest" and "o to Jail."

"It's Thursday," I said, after we caught him racing out through the window right when we got there one day. "He must be building a nest like them squirrels that got in our attic that time. Remember when they tore up that whole box of Daddy's old love letters from the army, and Mama got so mad?"

Course there wasn't really any *point* to his nest building, since there weren't any lady squirrels for him to impress.

"Unless he thinks the *Empress* is a lady squirrel," said Mary Al. "You know, like that mixed-up skunk in the cartoons?"

"Aw, he couldn't be *that* clueless, could he?" I asked.

And then we all looked at one another. "Yes, he could," we said together, and we busted out laughing.

I never seen J.D. so tickled over anything. "He must

think he's being charming when he chases her," she giggled. "And those pink candles—you think he's planning a candlelight dinner?"

Well, anyway, we all got a big kick out of it, once we saw what was going on. And the Empress was just too smart to let it bother her much. Seemed like she was getting smarter every day. She'd even learned to come if I whistled for her when it was time to go. You could tell she didn't really want to, even though I always gave her some kind of treat—raisins or peanuts or such. But she knew I'd be putting that leash on her again, was the thing. She looked so sad every time we left the island. It's hard to explain how a monkey looks sad, but when they do you can't miss it. Believe me, even their tails go limp.

She was still kind of shy with J.D., though that was getting a little better, too—I mean, at least she'd got to where she'd come up and take a grape out of her hand. But she wouldn't ever let J.D. actually *touch* her or anything, which hurt J.D.'s feelings, you could tell, even though she tried hard not to let on.

Mary Al thought she could help out by explaining her crying trick.

"It's real easy," she said. "Anybody can do it. You just put your mind on the saddest thing you can think of and scrooch up your face and start kind of gulping air, see? Come on, J.D., try it, it ain't a bit hard."

But J.D. just looked at her like she was out of her

mind. "I don't cry," she said. And that was the end of that.

Still, except for that one thing, and Thursday's various mental problems, these last couple weeks had been pretty near perfect. We were making the tree house better all the time. We'd got that tarp up on the roof, and I'd built us a little table, and we'd brought over some of them light-weight fold-up chairs and some more board games and a deck of cards. We even had us a Styrofoam cooler for our cold drinks.

Course all that equipment cut into my savings quite a bit, but I didn't really mind as long as I had enough left for my Phoenix trip. I just didn't feel right about asking Mary Al for money, though you'd think J.D. could have helped out a little more. But you know, for a rich kid she was sure short on cash. I guess Mrs. Monroe hadn't thought to give her an allowance—or maybe she was scared of what she'd do with it. All I know for sure is there ain't no way J.D. would've ever *asked*.

She did win a good many of our pennies, though. She was great at cards. She was teaching us crazy eights and canasta and hearts and boo-ray and gin rummy and spit in the ocean. I tell you what, it was real nice setting up there in the tree house like jungle explorers or something, drinking RC Cola and playing three-handed gin, with the leaves rustling all around us and the birds chirping away and our own private monkey swinging in every so often.

Just the peacefullest thing in the world. It had started seeming crazy to me that I'd ever actually *worried* about coming over here.

"Do you believe time travel is possible?" J.D. asks me out of the blue one day, not long after I'd mailed my letter to Danny.

"What?" I was trying to decide whether to discard my queen of hearts or that durn two of clubs I might need later. Didn't matter which one I chose, J.D. would end up winning, like she always did.

"Time travel. You know, E equals MC squared and all that. Einstein's theory of relativity."

"Oh," I said. I could feel my brain starting to ache already. "That." I took a deep breath and slapped down the two.

J.D. picked it up before it even had time to cool off. "Come on, you've been to the movies. You think one day we'll figure out how to bend time and space, like he said? So we can skip ahead to the future, or back a million years?"

"Lord, J.D., I don't know."

"I do," said Mary Al, rearranging her cards for the forty-seventh time. "I think it's possible." She handed a carrot stick to the Empress, who was perched on her shoulder, looking like she might start giving advice any minute.

I sighed. "Well, that settles it, then."

"I'm not kidding," said J.D. "I mean, if Einstein could believe it . . ." She discarded a red four. "I read this story about it once. About a guy who travels back in time to go dinosaur hunting."

"Like *Jurassic Park*?" asked Mary Al. She started to pick up the four, but just then the monkey shook her head and chittered, so she drew from the deck instead.

"Well, sort of. It starts out in the future, see, and they've just had this big close election, where some good guy candidate just barely beat out this evil person. And our main guy, he hears about it, and he's real glad. So then he buys this time travel vacation and goes off to the past to hunt dinosaurs. But not just *any* dinosaurs. He's only allowed to kill the ones that were about to die on their own, because if anything gets changed back there, it could mess up the future."

"Why would it mess it up?" I asked. "*Discard,* Mary Al. . . ."

"Well, just think about it. Say you kill the dinosaur that was supposed to be dinner for the saber-toothed tiger that was the great-great-zillion-great-granddaddy of the tiger that ate the zebra that otherwise would have kicked one of the Wright brothers in the head. We'da never had airplanes, get it?"

"Yeah, sure," I said. When she started talking this fast, there wasn't any sense trying to slow her down.

"So this guy in the story, they keep telling him to stay on the path and not mess anything up back there, because even just a little thing can make a big difference. But when the dinosaur starts coming, it scares him so bad he forgets the rules—he runs off the path and gets mud on his shoes. And everybody's mad at him, and he says aw, come on, it's just mud. Only what he doesn't know is there's this little tiny butterfly stuck in there. He's smushed it by acci-dent—he's killed it, you see—but he doesn't even notice it till he goes back to his regular time. And then he looks around, and everything seems *almost* the same. . . ."

Mary Al laid down the seven of hearts. "Almost?"

"Remember the big election? Where the good guy just barely beat the bad guy? Well, *now*—" J.D. cocked an eyebrow.

"The bad guy wins?" I took the seven and threw away that useless queen.

J.D. snapped it up. "Exactly," she said. "Gin rummy."

Well, it was only a story, was all, kind of cool and scary—just one of them things we'd get to talking about over in Elsewhere. I prob'ly would've never give it another thought, if it hadn't been for what come next. But an hour later Mary Al was still driving herself crazy over the whole idea.

"It don't make sense," she said, untangling the Empress's leash as she walked along. We'd already put up the boat by now and were on our way back to the big house.

"What doesn't make sense?" asked J.D. She was stooped over, picking dandelions.

"That story. If they're so smart in the future they can

send the guy back once, why don't they just send him back twice? Why don't they just go a half hour early and stop him before he runs? Then the butterfly don't get smushed and everything's okay."

I sighed and shook my head. "You're missing the point, Mary Alice. It's not supposed to be true like in real life, it's just supposed to make you think about stuff."

"No," said J.D. "She's right."

I stopped walking. "She's *right*?"

"See?" said Mary Al, sticking out her tongue at me.

"How is she right?" I asked, as we reached the house.

"Because if you can go back and mess things up, why can't you go back and fix things, too? They do it on 'Star Trek' all the time."

"Yeah, but that's just television."

"So?" She opened the back door to the storage room.

"I mean, it ain't supposed to be *real* or anything—"

"Joy? Are you down there?" It was Mrs. Monroe's voice, calling from the top of the inside stairs.

The wolf girl was back in a flash, hat or no. She didn't bother answering, just turned her back and carried her flowers over to the Empress's bowl.

"Yes, ma'am," I said. "We're here."

The old lady was already halfway down the stairs. "Telephone, Joy," she said.

No answer.

"Joy, I know you hear me. I said you have a telephone call."

J.D. swung around, green eyes snapping. "Forget it," she growled. "Who is it, old Nosy Rosy? I'm not talking to her again. I wouldn't talk to that witch if she was the last person on—"

But Mrs. Monroe was shaking her head. "It's not Dr. Rosenberg," she said real quiet. "It's your mother."

CHAPTER twenty-four

I didn't know if it was good news or bad news. I'm not even sure J.D. knew herself. She wasn't expecting it, though, I can tell you that much. The way she went so still all of a sudden—as if she'd been hit by a bullet and couldn't quite feel it yet—it made me want to shake her a little, check for blood, step in front of her some way before the next one hit.

She felt me and Mary Al and the Empress looking at her then. It jerked her awake, somehow. She gave us one of them *Mind your own business* glares and pushed past us, walking at first, then running, then all but bowling over her grandma as she pushed past *her,* too, and hurried out into the hall.

"Well, at least we know for sure now that her mama ain't *dead,*" said Mary Al, while we walked home. "That's good, right, Jim Junior?"

I nodded and said I guess, but all the rest of that day, I kept on wondering what the truth was. Was her mama sick or something? Something was wrong, it had to be. Else why was J.D. here for all this time? My folks didn't have a clue and the old lady wasn't talking and I couldn't just ask. I wasn't about to make *that* mistake again.

Course maybe it wasn't anything to worry about. Maybe her mom was just taking one of them long ocean cruises or some such. Maybe there was nothing more to it than that. But I couldn't get it out of my mind—all through lunch and while I was mowing the grass and even later over't Handy Dan, where I had to pick up some sandpaper and a can of varnish. It just kept pushing at me, the way J.D.'s face had changed when Mrs. Monroe said *your mother*.

"Mary Al! Jim Junior!" It was Daddy hollering from the TV room. "Y'all better come on down here and look at this nature show they got on channel eight. Might be something you could learn that would help you with your job!"

I was upstairs lying on my bed at the time, trying to do some reading to clear my brain, but I wasn't really having much luck with it. It was a book on our summer reading list that had been sitting on my shelf for six weeks—something called *The Time Machine*. I'd only thought of it now because of that time travel talk we'd had in the tree house this morning. I was thinking maybe this book would have some things in it I could tell J.D. about for a change.

But right off the bat in the very first sentence I run up against the word *recondite,* and by the time I got to *trammels* and *fecundity*—and I ain't even hit the second paragraph yet—I was feeling downright depressed.

So anyhow I didn't mind too much when Daddy hollered for us to come down and watch TV.

"It's all about monkeys," he explained when we got there. "Y'all look at this, now. It's real interesting."

Well, you know, it was a pretty good show—all about how these scientists are trying to help endangered species. Turns out they're running short of monkeys in the jungle, so the zoos all over the country are starting to train 'em up and send 'em back. They showed a whole bunch of different types, none that looked just like the Empress, but I guess I could have missed that part. There was golden monkeys and something called douc langurs and some little bitty cute ones named tamarins that looked just like minia- ture lions—Mary Al was crazy about those—and there was another part about orangutans, too, even though the man said they weren't really monkeys but apes. And all of 'em were in jungle training in one way or another.

It don't always work, though. The man was telling how some of the monkeys take right to it, and some don't, because they're just so used to being in cages and having their meals served up and all. But the ones that do, they learn how to be on their own and find plenty to eat and spend most their time in trees, which is good, because they're a lot safer up there. If they hang around on the ground, you see, there'll be all kinds of bigger animals, tigers and whatnot, that will eat 'em in a minute.

"So these *dumber* monkeys," I explained to J.D. next morning in the tree house, "they fail the course and have to stay in the zoo. But the *smart* ones, they do just fine, and after they graduate, the zoo ships 'em back to the Amazon or wherever in one of them nice preserves they got set up down there, where nobody can hurt 'em or shoot 'em or take 'em away to be pets. And then these smart monkeys meet others just like 'em, and they have little monkey babies, and pretty soon they ain't endangered anymore."

J.D. looked like she was only half listening. She was sitting at the table, scowling her old scowl, shuffling that deck of cards over and over again. She had tried to give the Empress a peanut, but Her Majesty had taken one look at her face and twitched her tail and gone skittering out the window. Which hadn't exactly improved J.D.'s mood.

Man, it was hot this morning. I wiped the sweat out of my eyes and tried again. "So what do you think, J.D.? If it was the Empress on that show, you think she'd pass?"

J.D. just shrugged. She wasn't paying me much mind, as I said before.

"Sure she would," Mary Al answered for her. "She's smarter'n any of them others!"

"Most intelligent of all the New World monkeys, right, J.D.? That's what the book said, remember?"

Bbrrrrrrrrt! went the cards.

"Maybe we ought to try and get the Empress in one

of them courses," said Mary Al. "I mean, just for a little while. I wouldn't want her to move down there for good or anything."

"I don't think it works like that, Mary Al. Once they go, that's it. It ain't like they're sponsoring monkey vacations."

"Well, they ought to. What if she's homesick? She might miss the Amazon sometimes, if her family's down there. Seems like they could at least let her go visit."

Bbrrrrrrrrrrrt! went the cards again. "She doesn't miss the Amazon," J.D. muttered. "She's never even been there."

Mary Al looked offended. "Yes, she has. Daddy says that's where she's from."

"Well, he's wrong, okay? Your daddy doesn't know everything. She comes from Houston, same as me."

I hated it when she got that tone, like she was so much smarter than the whole rest of the world. "How do you know that?" I asked.

She didn't answer right away, just sat there shuffling them cards. *Bbrrrrrrt! Bbrrrrrrrrt! Bbrrrrrrrrt!*

"How do you know?" I asked again.

A slimy little breeze slithered in the window, warm as dog breath and near as smelly. But better than no breeze at all, I guess. From somewhere away off far I could hear a kind of low grumbling that might have been thunder. I'd just about give up caring if J.D. ever answered or not, and then—

"Do you believe that time travel is possible?"

Aw, man, not *that* again. I wished I'd stuck with that book a little longer. "Come on, J.D. Who cares if it's possible?"

"Just answer the question."

"That ain't what I asked you—"

"I know what you asked me, now I'm asking *you*." She flung the cards at me—red queens and black kings and nines and threes and aces come flying through the air, scattering all over the place. And then she pushed her chair back and went to the window and stood there staring with her arms folded tight.

Me and Mary Al just sat there for a minute, too surprised to move. Not having a clue what to say. Out the window we could see the Empress playing hide-and-seek in the trees, and hear her happy-sounding chittering, while poor old crazy Thursday crashed around in the bushes, dodging acorns. . . .

And then just when I'd begun to think she'd turned to stone, J.D. started talking, real low—

"She never lived in the Amazon. I've seen her papers. She was born on a pet farm out I-45. This guy my dad used to play cards with bought her there. Old crazy Mo. He always took her with him every time he played—he thought she'd bring him luck, but she didn't. One night he just kept losing and losing, and my dad kept winning and winning, and finally Mo bet the monkey and Daddy won her, too. And he was glad, because he didn't think Mo treated her right."

J.D. stopped talking, and stared some more.

I started gathering up the cards. "So then your dad gave her to your grandma?"

The green eyes snapped my way. "He gave her to *me*. That same night. He brought her home and woke me up—he knew I wouldn't want to wait. And she came right to me. She wasn't afraid of me then." J.D. looked out the window again. "But they wouldn't let me keep her."

"Who wouldn't?" asked Mary Al.

"The apartment people, the place we were living. They didn't even allow cats, much less monkeys. Dad thought maybe we could hide her—I could've done it. But my mom got too nervous. She said it would just be asking for trouble."

She bit off a thumbnail and stood there chewing it for a while. It thundered again, no doubt about it this time.

I waited as long as I could stand it. The cards were piled up neat by now. "So that was when y'all thought of Mrs. Monroe?"

J.D. nodded. "It was her birthday, do you believe that? I didn't even know I had a grandmother. My dad and her—they never got along. And then all of a sudden he remembers it's her birthday."

"So he gave her the Empress."

"He thought she'd like it. He wanted it to be a surprise. He said she was all by herself in this big place, she ought to have a pet." J.D. shook her head. "My mom thought it was a bad idea—she said we ought to at least ask her first. But he kept telling her it would be all right. He said it was different now with the old man gone. He said we'd all make friends again and then I'd be able to visit the monkey anytime I wanted."

J.D. sat down and picked up the cards and went back to shuffling.

"So what happened?" Mary Al asked. "When y'all brought her over?"

J.D. kept her eyes on the cards. "She didn't want her. Anybody could see that. She didn't know what to say. So my dad said forget it, if she didn't like her, we'd give her to the zoo or something. But Granny said no, she never said she didn't like her, she was just surprised, was all. She'd have to find a cage and everything. And my dad said that shouldn't be too hard around here."

J.D. started laying out the cards for solitaire now, slapping them down real hard, one after another. "After that we just sat there, drinking iced tea. I never drank so much iced tea in my life. She kept making Jasper fill up my glass—it had so much sugar in it I wanted to gag. But I kept on drinking it, and we sat there and sat there, and finally my mom couldn't stand it anymore, she said we had to go. And Granny said but you just got here, aren't you staying for dinner? Only Mom was already halfway to the car by then, and we all got in and drove away."

J.D. kept turning over cards. "She was so mad. I didn't understand why she was so mad. My dad wanted to go to sleep because he'd been up late, but she wouldn't leave him alone, she kept telling him it was all so stupid and we shouldn't ever have come. And I was crying because we'd left the monkey, and then I had to go to the bathroom, and she said couldn't I wait, we'd be there in a minute. But I couldn't wait, I'd had all that iced tea, so I kept telling her I had to go, and Dad said for God's sake, pull over, Clarice, and she said okay, fine, and she jerked the wheel—"

J.D. had been talking a mile a minute, but she broke off there and wiped her nose and got up and went to the window and turned her back on us again. Her shoulders went up and down a couple times before she got 'em to hold still.

I didn't know what to say, so I didn't say anything.

More thunder. Louder this time. You could hear the wind picking up all around us, knocking the magnolia branches against the tree house. I felt it sway under my feet, just the tiniest bit.

I knew we ought to be leaving, but I couldn't move.

"So what do you think," she said, real low and bitter, "is time travel possible?"

Oh, man. So that's what she'd meant. No wonder she—oh, man, how could she stand it?

My insides ached, like I was catching the flu or something.

Mary Al looked a question at me, but I shook my head

and got up and went over by the window, too. "You can't be thinking like that, J.D. Stuff just happens, that's all. You can't go back in time and change it."

She wiped her nose again. "Just one thing," she said. "That's all it would take. Like the guy who stepped on the butterfly, remember?"

"That was only a story. Ain't nothing *you* could do—"

"I wouldn't have drunk the tea," she muttered. "I never even *liked* tea, don't you get it? If I just hadn't drunk all that stupid tea—"

Mama wouldn't have tried to pull over. . . . The car wouldn't have crashed. . . . My dad would still be alive. . . .

She didn't say any of it. Looked like she couldn't. She made a sort of strangled gulping sound and turned back to the window and tried to hide her face from me.

"J.D.," I said, "please don't cry. I'm real sorry about your daddy. Please, J.D., it wasn't your fault—"

I wished my mom was here to hug her or something and say go ahead, honey, you just cry it out. I wished anybody else was here. But it was just me and Mary Al, who looked scared to death, and I didn't know what to do, so I tried to kind of pat J.D.'s arm, but she jerked away like I'd burned her with a match. Somebody *help,* I wanted to yell, I ain't old enough. They never taught us this stuff in fifth grade—

And then all of a sudden, just like it had been a regular prayer and somebody handing out miracles before lunch, there was a blur of goldy brown fur swinging in the tree house window, and a soft chittering sound, and the Empress was there, she was sitting on J.D.'s shoulder and tending to her just the way she always done with Mary Al, petting her old tangly hair with them soft little fingers and planting little monkey kisses all over her face. And J.D. couldn't help herself then, she finally turned it loose, she cried just like a normal kid would do. While the thunder kept grumbling and the wind rose up again and rocked us in the tree house, she cried and cried and hugged that little monkey.

CHAPTER twenty-five

She eased up some, after a while. You know how you always do. First the hard sobs changed to that old jerky breathing, and then she got to that kind of trembly and embarrassed place. And by the time the first fat raindrops splatted against the magnolia leaves, she was even kind of halfway smiling, because the Empress was trying so hard to make her feel better.

Plus that fur and tail always tickled some, as I well knew.

Mary Al and me just kept quiet as long as we could, and tried not to stare or anything. Ain't nothing worse'n somebody staring at you at a time like that. But the weather was really starting to worry me now, so finally I had to clear my throat and speak up.

"J.D.? We probably better get going before this storm gets any worse. They're gonna be wondering where we are."

Mary Al looked a little nervous. "Can't we wait in here till it's over, Jimmy? You said you fixed the roof real good."

I shook my head. "No telling how long it'll rain. And it's way late already. If we don't get back pretty soon, they'll be sending out search parties."

"Well, let's go then," said J.D., wiping her nose again and starting out the door. "No sense standing around talking." She didn't really sound mad or anything—she was just trying to act like none of that other stuff ever happened. Though I noticed she didn't offer to let anybody else hold the monkey.

It wasn't raining too hard yet when we got to the boat, but I didn't much like the looks of them big black clouds. Still, I figured we could probably beat the worst of it, long as I put a little muscle in my rowing.

It thundered again, real low and grumbly.

"Maybe you better give the Empress to Mary Al, J.D."

J.D. shook her head.

"Well, just till we get the leash on her, anyway," I said, reaching in my pocket for it. "You know how she hates it when—well, shoot, where is it?"

"Where's what?"

"The leash. I know I had it right—oh, man. I must've left it in the tree house. It was bothering me when I sat on it, so I took it out of my pocket."

"Just forget it," said J.D. "I've got her. She's being real good."

But I was already climbing out of the boat. "We can't

just leave it—what would we tell Jasper? Y'all just wait here a minute, I'll be right back—"

I took off running then, splashing through the newborn puddles, not worrying much about how wet my shoes were getting. Wet wouldn't be any problem to explain on a day like this; it was time that was the trouble. But surely another five minutes wouldn't make all that much difference. Watch out now, I told myself, skidding through a muddy patch. Gonna break your leg if you ain't careful. Just another minute or so and you'll be—

BOOM! went the thunder, shaking the air all around me, making me jump about a mile. Lord, I wished we'd started back before this mess. But there was the tree, at least—I could see it just ahead, it was only another twenty yards, maybe—

When all of a sudden I spied that nut Thursday springing out the tree house window, then crashing off into the bushes when he seen me coming. Looked like he'd been up to his thieving ways again. What was that he'd got clamped in his teeth this time? Kind of trailing after him, whatever it was, long and brown and skinny and—

Oh, no, don't tell me—it couldn't be—it can't—it ain't really the *leash,* is it?

I doubled my stride and made it to the magnolia and clambered up to the tree house and looked all around. . . .

That leash was gone, no question.

"You crazy squirrel!" I leaned out the window and

hollered after him. "It's a *leash,* you dummy! What would you want with a stupid leash?"

But the lunatic burglar was long gone. By now he was probably sitting high and dry in his fool lover's nest, trying to braid it into booties or something.

I was about wore out by the time I got back to the boat.

"Where's the leash?" Mary Al asked.

"Thursday took it."

"Thursday took the *leash*?"

"That's what I just said, ain't it? Never mind, we'll think of something to tell 'em. Just hold on tight to the Empress, J.D."

We shoved off then—wasn't a second to spare. The rain was picking up pretty good now. And with every stroke of the oars seemed like it came down harder. By the time we'd reached the halfway point, you almost couldn't tell Lake Luly from the air above it. We were gonna need gills if this kept up.

Still, it didn't bother us as much it might have, it being so warm and all. Plus by now I figured there was no way we could get any *wetter.*

"Y'all all right?" I hollered.

"I'm all right," said Mary Al.

J.D. nodded, too. "We're fine."

And you know, she actually looked it. "We" being her and the Empress, you see. She'd pulled out her big old baggy T-shirt and got her tucked up under it somehow, like a frontways papoose—kind of like the way you see mothers carrying their babies at the supermarket. I swear, even with the two of 'em setting there sopping, she still seemed durn near happy as I'd ever seen her.

"I'm glad we lost the leash," she said. "She hates that stupid leash."

"What?" Mary Al hollered.

"I said I'm glad we lost the stupid—"

Krraacckka—BBLLLLAAAAAMMMMMMMM!!!

It happened so fast, I almost don't know how to tell it. It's all still pretty much one big blur in my head. One minute we're pushing along fairly steady through the waves, which are chopping up some but nothing I can't handle, and I'm rowing just as hard as I can, when that great big thunderclap comes *blamming* and scares us all to death. And then the monkey starts *yeeping* and gets away from J.D. and starts racing around the boat, so of course we all try to grab her, only somehow I lose an oar—it just slips right out of my hand—and while I'm trying to grab *that* the boat tips over—

And the next thing I know we're swallowing swamp water.

"Aaaaiieee—"

"Mary Al?"

"Where's the Empress? I can't find her—"

"*Mary Al!* Oh, God—"

"I can't *find* her—"

"Jimmy—*Jimmy!*"

"Mary Al? Here I am—hold onto me now—"

"Where's the Empress?"

"Yeep! Yeep! Yeep!"

"I've got her—hang on to the side, J.D.!"

"Is she okay?"

"She's okay—she's right here on my shoulder—just hang on, now, everybody's okay—"

But I was lying through my teeth. We weren't okay at all. We were in the biggest mess I ever been in, is what we were. Hanging on to our upside-down boat in the middle of Lake Luly. Which was either deeper than I thought or we'd hit one of them sinkholes, because I couldn't feel the bottom at all.

Kkrracckka—BOOOOOOMMM!

"Aaaiieee! Jimmy!"

"It's okay," I said again, trying to convince myself. "We're gonna be fine. Just don't panic, nobody panic—aw, come on, Mary Al, now ain't the time to *cry*—"

"I ain't crying—"

"Yes, you are—"

"Well, what if there's still gators in here?"

"There ain't any gators. For Pete's sake, Mary Al—"

"You think we can turn it back over?" asked J.D.

"We're gonna have to try. Come on, all together now, on the count of three. One . . . two . . ."

"Wait a minute, Jimmy, my hand's slipping—"

"You got it now?"

"No . . . wait . . . I think so—"

"Okay, let's try it again. You ready, J.D.?"

"Ready—"

"All right, then. One . . . two . . . Good Lord, what's that?"

The rain was so thick I could barely make it out—there on the main shore, over by the graveyard. It was some sort of giant shadow, and it was heading right straight for us. . . .

"It's Jasper!" cried Mary Al. "Hey, Jasper! Over here!"

I was never so glad to see anybody in my life.

"Over here!" everybody was hollering now, waving our arms just as hard as we could. "Help! Here we are! Right here, Jasper!"

Not that there was any doubt about him seeing us. He was coming at us like some kind of human freight train—wasn't about to let a little thing like water stand in his way. Lake Luly might as well been a mud puddle for all the mind he paid it. He just waded right in and kept on walking, didn't bother kicking off his shoes or any of that. Swimming now and again, but mostly he didn't have to—tall as he was, the old swamp never got much past his shoulders.

We had flipped over about midway between the island and the main shore—at least half a football field out in either direction. But I swear Jasper covered it in a third of the time it would have taken me to row. Before we knew it, he was gathering us up like so many half-drowned pups and righting that little boat and plopping us in it, one by one. He didn't act any too *pleased* about it—them big hands felt like steel cables around my middle when he lifted me. Not that I minded, all things considered.

He didn't climb in with us. Our oars were both gone now, anyway. He just got us settled and started walking back the way he'd come, hauling all of us along after him in the boat. All but the Empress, that is, who had wrapped herself around his neck like some kind of soggy muffler and wasn't about to let go.

I guess we must've been a pretty sorry-looking sight, all of us shivering and miserable, with our teeth knocking together and the rain pouring down on our heads. I don't know why it felt so much colder now. But I was too busy being grateful we were all still breathing to waste time worrying about anything else.

"Y'all okay?" I asked. "Didn't either of you get hurt anywhere, did you?"

Mary Al shook her head. "I'm o-k-k-kay," she said through her castanet choppers.

"What about you, J.D.?"

She didn't move, or look at me, even. She was sitting right across from me, staring into space.

"J.D.? You all right?"

Still she didn't answer. But now she turned her head my way, at least. She wasn't crying or anything. I guess she was done with that now. Seemed like the rain was crying for her, streaming down her face. And the look she gave me—it was almost as if she pitied me for even asking such a stupid question. As if any fool would know she'd never be all right again.

It wouldn't be ours anymore, she had said. *It wouldn't be Elsewhere, don't you get it?*

It thundered again, but not so close now. J.D. went back to staring into space.

Nobody said anything after that. Jasper dragged us along, and the rain kept pouring down. And even without turning around, when I looked in them sad green eyes, I could see the island, getting smaller and smaller.

III

LAST CHANCE

"Thank God," said Mrs. Monroe, when she opened the back door. The air coming out of the house was so cold, it smoked. "Where were you? What's happened? Where did you find them, Jasper?" Her questions came one on top of the other, spilling out of ghost-white lips. Looked like she'd bitten all the blood out of 'em, worrying. "But come in, come inside, you're wet to the skin—are they all right, Jasper? Are all of you all right?"

I didn't know what she kept asking *him* for, when we were right there. "Yes, ma'am," I said. "We're all just fine."

"Thank God," she said again. "Jasper, put that animal away and help me find dry things for these children. And for yourself, of course. There's that bureau in the blue room. . . . But what on earth . . . your mother called twice from work, she's on her way—"

Oh, Lord . . .

"But what happened? Where *were* you all this time?"

My mind started racing. What should we say? She didn't know—well, of course she didn't. Nobody knew where we'd been but us and Jasper. And he wasn't talking—

"We were on the island," said J.D.

I just about fell over. What are you doing? I thought at her, so hard she turned and gave me one of them pitying looks.

"What does it matter?" she said. "It's ruined, anyhow. You think he wouldn't have found some way to tell her?"

Meanwhile her grandma—who up till now had been leading us in through the storage room—had stopped dead still. "The island? But that's not possible."

J.D. looked her full in the face. "We've been going there for more than a month now. The storm hit while we were coming back and our boat turned over."

Mrs. Monroe went even paler. She couldn't seem to find her voice for a while. When she did, it had gone icy quiet. "You've been going to the island without my permission?"

I took a deep breath. "I'm sorry, Mrs. Monroe. We didn't think anybody would mind. We've mostly just been fixing things up over there."

"Fixing things? What things?"

"Just an old tree house. It was falling apart pretty bad, so we thought—"

She took a step back, as if I'd slapped her. "You had no right," she said, in that terrible low voice. "No right . . ."

"I'm real sorry, Mrs. Monroe—"

"You shouldn't have even *been* there, do you understand?" She looked at J.D. again. "A boat, you said. What boat?"

J.D. shrugged. She was done talking, I guess.

"Just an old rowboat," I said. "We found it in a toolshed."

"And this has been going on for more than a month?"

"Yes, ma'am."

Mrs. Monroe turned on Jasper, who was still right behind us. "How did this happen? Why wasn't I informed?"

Informed? What did that mean? Informed about *us?* Jasper was supposed to be *watching* us? Since when? Since forever? I looked at J.D., but she might've been a block of wood. Dead eyes, dead everything, dead, dead, dead.

But her grandma—for all her fine manners—was mad as spit, waiting for Jasper to answer her whatever way he could. Course he didn't say anything—that is, not with his mouth, and not with his hands or his face, either. He just stood there looking real calm and, well, *dignified,* if that's the right word. I mean, if a person can look dignified with a monkey hanging on to his neck. But the Empress was nervous enough for both of them. He was stroking her head, to keep her quiet, while her goldy brown eyes kept darting from him to the hell-eyed old lady.

"They could have been killed." Her voice was shaking. "Don't you realize that? God in Heaven, it's a wonder they weren't all killed."

"No, ma'am," I said. "It ain't Jasper's fault. He was there just in time—he saved our lives, is what he done."

I think maybe she heard me then. She looked at me, at least. And then she looked at Mary Al, who was pretty near blue with cold by this time, and she put an arm around her shaking shoulders. "These children are freezing. Jasper, take care of James, please. You come with me, Mary Alice."

Mary Al looked back at me, scared to death. I nodded at her. *It's all right, she ain't gonna hurt you, just go on.*

"Joy—" Mrs. Monroe turned to J.D. last, expecting the usual snarling and hissing, I guess. But the wolf girl was gone now. There was nobody left but this person made of wood. "Go to your room and get changed," said her grandma. "We'll discuss this later."

J.D. didn't say anything, just started to go.

"J.D.?" I called after her.

She turned around and waited. *What's the use?* the dead eyes asked.

"See you later," I said, when I couldn't think of anything else.

But she looked at me like she hardly even knew me and walked away.

🌳

The storm had pretty near blown itself out by the time Mama got there. The actual *rainstorm,* that is. Parentwise, the heavy weather was only just getting started.

"They did *what*?" Daddy hollered, when Mama told him. She'd already given us the whole lecture on the way home, but now we got it from two sides at once:

"I thought you had better sense, son—"

"Ought to be ashamed—"

"Meddling in places you never belonged—"

"Fooling around with old boats—"

"And not a life jacket in sight! How many times have I told you—"

"A wonder they weren't all drowned—"

"What if something had happened to your little sister?"

"She's not but seven years old—"

Daddy looked at me like he'd never been so disappointed in anybody. That was the worst of it. Not the yelling so much. I figured I had that coming. He shook his head and put his hand on his back like it was paining him again. "So you got yourself fired, I guess?"

Me and Mary Al had mostly just been staring at our muddy shoes, waiting till the mad part was over. Well, she was blubbering some, but no more'n what you'd expect. But now we both looked up.

"Fired?" I repeated. "No sir, nobody said anything about firing us—"

"Not fired, exactly," said Mama. She'd pretty much had her say by now—looked like she was ready to ease up just a little bit. "Mrs. Monroe thinks some time apart might be a good idea, that's all."

Daddy shook his head again. "They've been fired,

Maggie. And rightly so. No sense calling a mule a music teacher."

"But we never meant to hurt anything—it was only an accident—"

"We can't be fired," wailed Mary Al. "What about the Empress? She won't understand if we don't come no more!"

"I imagine she'll get over it," said Daddy.

Well, Mary Al really went to moaning and hollering then, and I can't say I blamed her. Mama was right—she wasn't but seven, wasn't any of this her fault. I was the one in the wrong, not her. But she was taking it awful hard, just the same.

And there wasn't any little monkey gonna swing in here to cheer her up.

CHAPTER twenty-seven

The big black gate stayed shut tighter'n ever the next two rotten weeks. That was about as putrid a fourteen days as you will find anywhere. Daddy and Mama got over being mad at me after the first few—they just grounded me until further notice, was all—and they pretty much let Mary Al off the hook. But she was still moping around missing the monkey, and I couldn't help feeling sort of sunk-down and good for nothing, myself.

My mind just wouldn't stop running back to J.D.'s crazy time travel talk, was the thing. Like to drove myself nuts, going over all the little pieces had to fit together so perfect to ruin that day the boat tumped over. If the storm had only held off another half hour, if that durn fool Thursday hadn't stole the leash, if it hadn't thundered *quite* so loud and I hadn't dropped the oar. . . .

Course if we'd never gone to the island in the first place, we might've avoided the whole mess altogether. But somehow that seemed like the worst solution of all. My brain always skipped right past it and kept harping on the same old question: If I could go back and do it all over again, what would I change?

Oh, sure, I should've seen to it we had life vests. Daddy'd pounded that in my head my whole life. And the sneaking around wasn't anything I was proud of. But had it really been so terrible, fixing up that old tree house?

"Jasper must not have thought so," I said to Mama. My bicycle tire had sprung a leak and I was out in the carport trying to put a cold patch on it only the durn thing wouldn't hold and then my hand had slipped and I'd torn a fingernail down to the quick so then I hollered and Mama come out to see if I was okay and somehow we ended up sitting on boxes, talking about the Monroes.

"Jasper?" Mama looked confused. "What does Jasper have to do with it?"

"Well, he must've seen us over there—turns out she had him watching us the whole time. That's why he was there so quick when we had our trouble. But we didn't know it, till Mrs. Monroe got so mad at him for not telling on us sooner."

"He knew you'd been going to the island?"

"Sure, he did. He knows everything. I bet he used to look out for J.D.'s daddy the same way. I bet he was *glad* we were fixing the tree house—else why didn't he stop us? It wasn't no good to anybody the way it was, Mama. I don't see why Mrs. Monroe should mind so much."

Mama was quiet for a minute, thinking this over. "This tree house—you think Joy's daddy built it?"

I nodded. "A real long time ago. It was in terrible shape. And all we did was *fix* it, Mama—you wouldn't believe what a good job we done. . . ." My throat went all cloddy, thinking how great it had been—our table and chairs and that nice little ice chest and everything. I wondered was the deck of cards still sitting where we left 'em, or if Thursday had taken up solitaire by now.

My fingernail was throbbing again. I squeezed on it, trying to make it stop. "There just wasn't any reason for her to get so mad about it."

Mama took my hurt finger in her hands and blew on it for a while. Then she gave it back to me real easy. "He was her little boy, that's all. No matter what happened between them later."

"Who was?"

"Max Monroe. When he built that tree house." She shook her head and smiled a little. "Isn't that just always the way? They'd given him a whole castle, but all he wanted was some old scrappy tree house he could build himself." She leaned over and fake-punched my arm. "Remember the Christmas we gave you that fine croquet set, and you never played with any of it but the box it came in?"

Lord. The croquet set. How could I forget? I'd been hoping for a dartboard that year, or maybe even an ant farm. "Well, it was such a nice *big* box. . . ."

She chuckled. "It's okay, honey, I'm nearly over it." And then she said, real soft, "That poor old woman."

"Mrs. Monroe?" I'd never really thought of her as *poor*.

But Mama was nodding. "She must've watched him build that tree house. It must just about kill her to see it now, or even to think about somebody else touching it. Why, if anything ever happened to you—" She held up her hands and shook her head hard, like she was trying to push the thought away. And then she took a deep breath, and let it out, and smoothed down that place in my hair, like she always does. "He was her little boy, Jimmy. You just can't imagine. . . . You don't know yet what that does to a person's heart."

Mama had to go back in the house after that, and I stayed out there fooling with the cold patch till I finally got it right. But for the next few days I kept thinking about what she'd said. Was that really all there was to it, then—the whole big mystery of the island? Why the old lady had torn down the bridge instead of fixing it? I thought about her face that morning when she'd found J.D. wearing the old coat. I'd pushed that out of my mind, but it was all the same, wasn't it? The tree house and her boy's old room and even the monkey—she'd locked 'em all up where she wouldn't have to see 'em and go to hurting again.

Only then *we* come along, didn't we?

I wondered how J.D. was making out these days, cooped up over there with that sad old straight-backed lady. Did they ever let her help with the monkey now? Was she still carved out of wood? Was she holed up in her room, with the wolf hat on her head? I asked Mama to look for her when she went over for her work, but she said she never saw her at all, and Mrs. Monroe was so quiet and stern she couldn't find a way to ask.

So anyway, these fourteen rotten days just dragged theirselves on and on, and I worried about it all till I was sick of worrying. And then at quarter to nine on a hot sunshiny Friday in August, two weeks to the day after we got fired, things finally started looking up a little.

"Jim Junior!" Mama called to me from the front door. "Come here, honey—I got something for you!"

I was still sitting at the kitchen table eating my egg on toast. "What is it?" I hollered back, not moving. Just didn't have the energy, somehow. I'd woke up thinking about the tree house again. Had I thought to leave that door pulled tight? Them new hinges were gonna rust if nobody was there to keep 'em oiled up. . . .

"Come *here,* Jimmy! I'm gonna be late to Mrs. Monroe's, as it is—"

She was due there again, was she? Well, maybe she'd get a glimpse of J.D. this time. Maybe I could send her a message or something. Even if I didn't have any idea what to put in it. . . .

I sighed and went to the door. "Yes, ma'am?"

Mama was grinning. "I think you might like this." She put a letter in my hand.

My heart gave a big old happy jump. "Danny? It's from Danny?"

She nodded and smiled while I ripped into it. "That nice Terri Ashley brought it over—she and her husband just moved in to the Brophys' old house. She said the letter's been sitting there a week, but Marty forgot to tell her. Looks like Danny got mixed up and wrote his old address on it instead of ours!"

Man, oh, man. My hands were all jerky, I was so excited, plus Danny'd put about a ton of Scotch tape on the envelope. But finally I got it open:

Yo Jamesolini,

I got your letter. So whazzup, dude, you ever coming out here or what? My mom says anytime before school starts, we can maybe even go to the Grand Canyon and the House of Wax both. I went with this guy Deano Levin 3 times already, it was really gross you'd love it. Phoenix is great, well pretty hot but you know me, I'm cool so it's no problem. Well, I gotta go, we're going to Goony Golf and then get pizza, hurry up and come and we'll do that, too.

Your old bud,
Daniel S. Brophy

P.S. What's the deal with this Monroe job? Are you kidding me? What do you do there, hunt vampires? Does the old lady sleep with a stake through her heart?

Write me back,
The Broph

"Good news?" Mama asked.

"Better'n anything. He wants me to come out there as soon as I can."

"Oh . . . well, that's nice, sweetheart. But I wouldn't—well, we'll talk about it when I get home, okay? I've got to run now, I'm already late." She gave me a quick kiss. "It's good to see you smiling," she said, and rushed off.

Man, oh, man. Good old Danny. He sure knew how to cheer a person up. Now, that was what I call a great letter. I was just reading it over for the fourth time in a row when Daddy came downstairs. He was all decked out in his good suit and everything. He didn't wear it a whole lot—I remember one time he put it on to go to a funeral and Ranger didn't know who he was and nearly bit him—but he was supposed to have his second interview over at Wal-Mart in the hardware department this morning.

"Is your mother gone yet?" He was trying to get his tie straight and having some trouble with the knot.

"Yessir, she just left."

"Well, shoot. Gonna have to tough it out, I guess." He saw the letter then. "Hear from your friend?"

"Yessir," I said. "He wants to know when I'm coming to Phoenix. He says it's okay with his mom."

"Well, that's real nice of her." He loosened the knot and started over. "Did you ever save up enough money for your ticket?" He wasn't rubbing it in or anything. He knew how bad I felt about losing the job. He was just asking, is all.

"I don't know, I hope so. I was thinking I could ride my bike down to Travel Unlimited and see what kind of deal Aunt Betsy could get me."

"How much do you have?"

"Ninety-eight—no, wait—" I took my wallet out of my pocket and double-checked. "Ninety-seven sixty-nine."

Daddy shook his head. "I don't know, son. Depends on how far in advance and all. Maybe it's enough, but you don't want to get your hopes up too high."

Well, it was a little late to be telling me that. They were already way *up* there, was the thing. "Yessir, I know, but I was thinking, if I'm twenty bucks short or something, I could probably earn it pretty quick mowing lawns. I mean, when I'm not grounded anymore. . . ."

Daddy looked at me for a minute, like he was thinking that over. "Well," he said finally, "I guess you're done with that now. You made a mistake, and you learned from it, so we'll call it even. How's that?"

"That's great. Thanks, Daddy."

"You're welcome. And I tell you what, I'll make you

a proposition. If this Wal-Mart job works out like I hope it will, and you'll take care of any extra little chores come up around here in the next couple weeks, I'll spot you the twenty or whatever extra it takes to buy that ticket. Is that a deal?"

I couldn't believe my good luck. I would've hugged him, if I hadn't been so old. "Yes, *sir!*" I said, and we shook hands on it.

I was all set to rush out the door right then, but Daddy said, "Hold on, son, you're forgetting about your little sister. Didn't your mama ask you to keep an eye on her until I get back?"

"Oh," I said. "Yessir." It had slipped clear out of my head. "But maybe she'll want to ride with me—would that be okay?"

"You could always just call, couldn't you?"

"Yessir, but I wanted to look at their brochures and all that. They might have one about special stuff to do while you're in Arizona."

Daddy thought about it. "Well, you'd have to watch her real good. She hasn't been riding as long as you. Y'all don't have to cross any busy streets going that way, do you?"

"No sir, it's just over there on Kinsel Drive. We'll be real careful."

"Well, I guess that'll be all right." Daddy gave his tie one last tug. He had it lumped up kind of peculiar to one side. "This thing look funny to you?"

"No sir, it looks real slick."

He grinned and clapped me on the back. "Thanks, sunshine. You don't lie worth a hoot, but I appreciate it. I'll see you later, then."

So he went on, and I ran into the TV room and rousted out Mary Al, who was sitting in there watching that cartoon where Bugs Bunny calls the square dance and has all them old country boys acting so silly. It's one of the best ones, but she wasn't even cracking a smile. I swear, she'd been lower'n puddle mud herself, these last two weeks.

She perked up some when I told her we were gonna go bike riding, but not enough to make her hurry or anything. You never seen anybody take so long to put on her shoes.

"Come on, Mary Al, me and Danny both be dead of old age by the time you get them laces tied."

"I'm coming. Just got a durn knot, that's all."

"Oh, for Pete's sake. Here, let me. You got to do it the way I showed you, remember? Always start with the left one *first* and then—"

Bbrring!

Well, shoot. I didn't have time to fool around answering the telephone.

Bbrring!

"I'll get it!" Mary Al started to twist her foot out of my hand.

"No—hold on a minute now, you're gonna trip. Pretend we already left. Whoever it is can just call back later."

Bbrring!

"Jimmy—"

"Aw, it ain't gonna be for either one of us. Just somebody trying to make an appointment with Mama. Ain't nobody but Conrad Smith called me since Danny left."

Bbrring!

But wait a minute—what if it was Danny? Could be there was something he forgot to tell me in his letter. Better not take any chances.

I jumped up and ran to the phone.

Bbrri—

"Hello?"

There was a weird clicking noise in my ear—sounded like a bad connection or something.

"Jim?"

"Danny? I can't hardly hear you."

"Who's Danny?" the voice growled. "This is J.D."

CHAPTER twenty-eight

My heart did one of them big wild jumps again. Up or down, I really couldn't tell you.

"J.D.? What's wrong? Why do you sound like that?"

"Like what?"

"Like you're sitting in a submarine."

"Oh. That's just because of this stupid pay phone."

"Pay phone? What are you doing on a pay phone?"

"I can't explain right now. I just need you to come down here, okay? Corner of—hold on a minute—Kansas and Fourth. And bring five dollars. Well—six if you can spare it. Six bucks, you got that? I'll pay you back later."

"What do you need six bucks for? What's going on, J.D.?"

"I told you, I'll explain when you get here. Just *get here,* Jimmy. Come *now.* I need you, okay? Kansas and Fourth. And don't tell anybody."

"Wait a minute, J.D. Kansas and Fourth—ain't that the—"

Click! went the phone.

"The bus station?" I finished, as the dial tone buzzed in my ear.

Good God almighty . . .

"What's the matter?" asked Mary Al. "Is something wrong with J.D.?"

"I don't know. I hope not. Doggone crazy girl . . . Come on, Mary Al, give me your foot. Ain't no time to fool around."

"We still gonna go see them pictures of the Grand Canyon?"

"No," I said, bending down and untangling that knot and tying her tennie in two seconds flat. "There's been a change of plans."

We had to cross not just one but five busy streets getting to Kansas and Fourth, but I didn't see any way around it. I couldn't leave Mary Al at home by herself, and I couldn't just not go. Not with old J.D. about to—about to *what*? Hop some fool bus to Argentina?

"Come *on*, Mary Al. You got to pedal harder."

"I'm pedaling hard as I can—"

Shoot. I could have been there ten minutes ago if I'd been by myself. This was like some kind of torture— like one of them dreams where you're trying to run, but your legs have turned to concrete and the twelve-eyed monster behind you is getting closer and closer. . . . Just don't do anything stupid, J.D. I'm coming, okay? I'm coming. . . .

We stayed on the sidewalks as much as we could. I know that ain't the rule, but the cars whizzing by us made me nervous for Mary Al. Looked like everybody just wanted to get out of this part of town fast as they could. Not that I blamed 'em. It was all kind of slouched-down and cut-rate-looking—used car lots and a couple scroungy barbecue joints and some beat-up houses with signs in the windows: PALMS READ, MONEY BACK IF WE'RE WRONG and MURRAY'S COTTAGE CHEESE CEILING REMOVAL and YES! WE HAVE PETRUS RABBIT FEED. . . .

How had J.D. got down here? I wondered. She must've walked, I guess. She didn't have a bike, and Jasper wouldn't have dropped her off in this neighborhood. Aw, man, that durn fool girl. What was she up to now? You stop thinking about her for five minutes and look what happens.

"There it is," I said finally, pointing up ahead. "That's the driveway on the left—turn in right there."

"Where's J.D.?"

"I don't know. By the pay phones, I guess. You think they'd have 'em inside or—"

"Over here!"

She was standing in a little alleyway at the side of the building—not the window side or the bus side but just a solid gray concrete wall over on the left.

"Good Lord," I muttered, "is she wearing a *coat*?"

Sure enough, she was. It must've been at least ninety

degrees already, even at ten in the morning, but she had on that outsize overcoat again—the one we'd seen her wearing that other time in her daddy's old room.

"What's wrong, J.D.?" I asked, even before I climbed off my bike. "You didn't buy a ticket or anything, did you? You ain't actually thinking about—"

"Shh!" she said, waving us over and ducking back into the alley, like this was some kind of big-deal mystery movie. "Did you bring the six bucks?" she asked, soon as we caught up.

"I ain't giving you any six bucks. Not unless you tell me what you need it for. What are you doing here, anyway? And why are you wearing that coat?"

She didn't answer right away. She looked all around first, like she was making sure nobody was watching. And then she opened the coat to show us something—something little and furry with big goldy brown eyes looking at us and long arms hanging on tight around her middle.

"The Empress!" Mary Al gasped.

"Shh!" said J.D. "I don't want anybody to see her."

"Why not?"

"Because they don't allow monkeys on buses, that's why not."

"Aw, man, J.D., you ain't gonna take her on the *bus*—"

She wasn't listening. She checked all around again, then got the Empress the rest of the way out and handed her to Mary Al, who laughed and cried and hugged her and carried on. Looked like she had on a brand-new collar and leash—J.D. had run it through her coat sleeve so it wouldn't show—and a little pair of them paper diapers that babies wear.

I shook my head. "This is crazy, J.D. What's she wearing them baby pants for? And how long have you been carrying her under that coat? She'll suffocate under there."

"No, she won't. I let her out every chance I get. And the diapers are just for the trip, that's all. Anyhow, the coat's not as hot as it looks—I took out the lining. And I brought her a big water bottle, and I even cut air holes, see?" She stretched out the coat some more to show us.

Sure enough, there were four or five neat little triangles sliced out of the nubby brown material—which still looked plenty hot to me, lining or no.

"So what's the deal, anyhow? You two gonna run away and join the circus?"

J.D. got quiet for a second. Then—"I'm not running away. I'm going home."

That shut me up. But finally I managed, "You mean, to your mom's?"

She shrugged. "Yeah, sure. I said home, didn't I? What else would I mean?"

"But your grandma—Jasper—they'll be worried sick—"

"No, they won't. He took the car to get rewired or something. She's getting her hair done. By the time they notice I'm gone, I'll already be there. I'll call from my mom's—what's wrong with that?"

"I don't know, it's just—well, if you're just going

home, why do you have to sneak around on buses? Why can't you just ask your grandma to have Jasper drive you over when he gets back?"

"Because I'm not leaving without the Empress, okay? I'm not leaving her sitting down there in that cage. She hates it, Jimmy. She hates it worse than ever now that she knows about the island."

"Aw, J.D., she's just a monkey. You don't have any way of knowing what she's thinking—"

"Don't tell me what I know." The green eyes snapped at me. "You ought to see how she looks every day when I go down to walk her around. Jasper's been letting me— he bought her the new leash. She gets so excited, she thinks I'm gonna take her to the island. But of course I can't— the boat's gone now. And when I take her back to her cage, she just looks so *disappointed,* Jimmy. She's not even eating right anymore—she's losing weight—can't you tell? She's gonna get sick, I know she is. She's awful weak already. If we don't do something, I'm afraid she might die."

"What?" Mary Al cried, hugging the Empress tighter than ever. "She can't die!"

Aw, man. She did look skinnier, didn't she? And I'd never seen her acting so quiet. . . . And it was all our fault, wasn't it? If she'd never been to the island, she'da never known what she was missing. . . .

"But how's taking her with you to Houston gonna help, J.D.? You got another island over there?"

J.D. shook her head. "I'm not taking her home. I told you, they won't let her stay there. I'm gonna enroll her in one of those jungle training programs at the Houston Zoo."

Mary Al's eyes opened wide. "You mean like we saw on the television?"

J.D. nodded. She stroked the Empress's head, real easy. "She'll love it, I know she will. She'll be the smartest one. We got her half-trained already. Think how happy she'll be in a real rain forest—it'll be just like the island, only better. And she'll have friends—she can have a whole family. She won't ever be lonesome again."

"But how do you know they'll let her in? In the training program, I mean? Did you call over there?"

"I tried about a thousand times. You can't get through. All you get is one of those stupid recorded messages. I've got to just *take* her, that's all. Once they see her, they'll know how to help her. It's their *job*, Jimmy—it's the *zoo*, for Pete's sake. They have to take care of animals—that's what they're *there* for."

"I don't know, J.D.—"

"Well, we don't have time to stand here talking about it till you do. You gonna lend me the six bucks or not?"

"For your ticket?"

J.D. nodded. "I thought I had enough—it's just ninety miles, one way. But they're asking fifteen bucks, do you believe that?"

I still didn't know what to say, so I just stood there.

"I got money at home," Mary Al piped up. "Mama's been putting it up for me in her top drawer. I could run back there and get it—"

J.D. shook her head. "Thanks, but there's no time. The bus leaves in twenty minutes." She looked at me again.

"I don't know, J.D. The Empress ain't yours—"

"She should have been. My dad gave her to me first. Everything else—it was all just a mistake."

"But what'll your grandma say?"

"She'll be glad to be rid of her. She never wanted her in the first place. I'll just say I took her out and she ran away. It's not like it never happened before."

"But Jasper—he's crazy about her. He'd feel real bad if he lost her—"

"He'd feel worse if she was dead. Anyway, Jasper doesn't own her. How could anybody *own* her? She's the Empress— she's not some *thing*. Just *look* at her, Jimmy—"

I looked. She seemed . . . kind of limp, is the only way I can describe it. And them big eyes—they seemed almost *too* big now, and kind of tired, somehow, like she'd given up caring what happened.

I wiped the sweat out of my own eyes. My head was spinning again. "I don't know, J.D.—"

"Will you stop saying that? What is there to know? She'll *die* in that cage. Isn't that enough?"

Still I just stood there. I felt sick to my stomach. My heart was pounding so loud I couldn't hear myself think.

And then I took a deep breath and started to pull out my wallet. "You're sure your mom knows you're coming? You've talked to her?"

The green eyes turned to slits. "Sure I talked to her. I talk to her all the time. What do you think, I don't talk to my own mother?"

"I didn't say that. I was just wondering, is all. . . . She's meeting you at the station, then?"

"She doesn't have to meet me. I can take care of myself. I know my way around Houston. I'm not some baby."

"So she *don't* know you're coming, is that what you're saying?"

"Sure she knows. She *wants* me to come. I told you already." J.D. kicked the side of the building. "She just doesn't know I'm coming right now, that's all."

"Well, why not? Why can't you just call her up?"

"None of your business, that's why not. There's reasons, okay? Just give me the six bucks, Jimmy."

I put the wallet back in my pocket. "No," I said. "I can't let you do it."

"What do you mean, *let* me?"

"I mean I'm not gonna give you the money. It's too dangerous."

For a few seconds J.D. just stared at me, like she couldn't believe she'd heard me right. Then all of a sudden she shrugged. "Okay, forget it."

I wasn't sure I understood. "Forget what? Forget the whole thing, right? You're not going?"

"Just forget it, okay? Here, Mary Al, give the Empress to me."

Mary Al didn't want to, but J.D. took her back, anyway—the Empress was too limp to resist—and started buttoning the big coat over her again.

"So are you saying you're going back to the mansion or—"

"I'm saying forget it, that's all. Forget you ever saw me. Forget I ever asked. I thought you were my friend, but I was wrong."

"I am your friend."

She stopped buttoning and glared at me, as if I'd said it just to spite her. I couldn't even hardly believe I'd said it myself. Wasn't any *choosing* to it. All of a sudden it was just a pure fact, like having brown eyes or being a sucker for a knuckleball.

"I'm your friend, J.D."

"Yeah, right," she muttered. And she turned around and walked away.

I followed right after her, Mary Al dogging my every step. "I just don't think it's a good idea, that's all. Or safe, even—you going over there to that big city without somebody meeting you. I can't let you get on that bus all by your—"

I broke off. She was heading into the station, for some reason.

"Where are you going? You don't have enough money—what do you think you're doing?"

She didn't answer me. She walked right over to the waiting room benches and stopped in front of a skinny lady who was reading one of them paperback romances. "Excuse me, ma'am," she said, real humble, "I'm sorry to bother you, but I lost my lunch money and I was wondering if you had any change to spare."

The lady started shaking her head before she even looked up. You could see the words *Not today* all set to come out of her mouth. But then her eyes run right into J.D.'s stomach—which was stuck out pretty far because of the covered-up Empress—and all of a sudden her face changed. "Maybe I have a little something," she murmured, looking all embarrassed. And then she riffled through her purse and came out with a dollar.

"Thank you, ma'am," said J.D.

"You take care of yourself, honey," said the lady.

Good Lord. Did she think J.D. was—oh, good Lord. I could feel my face getting all hot. *"J.D.,"* I whispered, as loud as I could. Me and Mary Al were kind of hanging back from her now, as you might suspect. "J.D., *stop* that, for crying out loud." But she never even looked at me, just moved right on to the next bench, where a pimply-faced soldier was eating a bag of cheese puffs.

"Excuse me, sir," she started. . . .

I couldn't stand it anymore. I walked up to her real fast and grabbed ahold of her arm. *"Stop* it, do you hear me?" I muttered, pulling her along with me to the ticket window. "You win, okay? Just don't ever do that again."

She opened the green eyes all wide and innocent. "Do what, James Henry? You're not blushing, are you?"

"Cut it out, J.D. I swear, I'll—"

"May I help you?" asked the ticket man.

I cleared my throat. "Do you still have room on the next bus to Houston?"

"If you hurry. Plenty of room on the ten-thirty express. Traveling with or without parents?"

"Without."

"Will you be needing a return? Express only for unaccompanied children, and no travel after dark, no exceptions."

"Is there an express coming back from there before dark?"

He checked his schedule. "There's one leaves Houston at five o'clock, arrives here at six-thirty."

"Okay, then—" I took a deep breath. In my mind I could see a little gold map of Arizona, flying away on cartoon wings. "Give me three round-trip tickets to Houston, please."

CHAPTER twenty-nine

It was almost worth losing my trip to Phoenix to see J.D. standing there staring at me, all slack-jawed, for once in her life. Only *almost,* which Daddy says don't count 'cept in horseshoes and hand grenades, but at least it was better than nothing.

"What do you think you're doing, Jimmy?" she hissed in my ear, as I counted out ninety dollars from my wallet.

"Shut up. I'm buying our tickets."

"What do you mean, *our* tickets? *I'm* the one going, not you. And I don't need a round trip, either. I'm not coming back."

I handed the man the cash. "It's my money, I'll take that chance."

"But why? This is crazy. I don't need you to—"

"Don't tell me what you need. You don't know what you need. You think—"

The man handed me the three tickets and tried to look like he hadn't heard a word. Which I appreciated.

I mumbled thank you and grabbed ahold of J.D. and Mary Al—one elbow apiece—and pulled 'em past the candy machines and the toilets and over to the wall of pay phones.

"You think I'm gonna stand here watching while you go off half-cocked to Houston with a sick monkey under your coat? Once I see you sitting at your mama's, I'll eat that extra half ticket, no problem. But we're gonna have it ready, just in case."

"Who do you think you are, my &*%# baby-sitter?"

"Watch your mouth, Joy Dolores. This ain't just about you, remember? If the Empress is sick, it's my fault as much as anybody's. She never asked us to take her to the island. Anyhow, I wouldn't even *have* the stupid money if it wasn't for her. I figure fair is fair, that's all."

Mary Al tugged on my arm, all excited. "Can we ride that little train when we get to the zoo, Jimmy? Like we done last time when Daddy took us?"

"For Pete's sake, Mary Al. This ain't a *pleasure* trip."

There was a crackling noise out of the speaker system. "The ten-thirty express to Houston is now boarding at gate three. Please proceed to gate three for departure at exactly ten-thirty."

I looked at my watch. Ten-twenty-one. "Y'all better go on to the bathroom or whatever you have to do. It's an hour and a half to Houston. I'll be waiting right here— I gotta make a phone call."

J.D.'s eyebrows shot up. "Who're you calling?"

"My daddy. He'll be back by now, wondering where we are."

"What are you gonna tell him?"

"I don't know yet. Y'all just go on, okay?"

J.D. looked at me a second. Then she nodded. "You'll think of something."

Yeah, right, I thought, as they disappeared into the ladies' room. But not necessarily something *smart* . . .

I reached in my pocket again and started scrabbling around for a quarter. I couldn't even believe what I was about to do. It felt just like one of them out-of-body deals they have on "Geraldo." You know, when a person gets struck by lightning or something and everybody thinks they're dead, and all the time they're just floating up above theirselves, watching the whole thing? I swear, it felt just like that.

See Jimmy finally find his quarter. See him pick up the phone and put the quarter in. See him dial his own number and stand there waiting while it rings three times. See his eyebrows start to sweat when his daddy says—

"Hello?"

"Daddy?"

"That you, Jim?"

"Yessir—"

"Everything all right? Y'all still at the travel place?"

"No sir—I mean, everything's fine, but we ain't there."

"Well, where are you then?"

"We, uh, me and Mary Al just got invited to go to the zoo over in Houston. You think that'd be all right?"

I could hear Daddy clearing his throat. He always does that when he don't know what to say. "Well, I don't know, Jimmy. Your mama's not home yet. Maybe we better wait and check with her first."

"We can't wait, Daddy—they're leaving right now. I really don't think she'd mind. It ain't a long trip or any-thing—we'd be home before dark."

"Well, now, just wait a minute, son—who is it that's invited y'all, anyway?"

See Jimmy's lips go dry. See him take a deep breath. See him open his mouth and tell the biggest lie of his entire life—

"Well, you know how Mama's been wanting us to be better friends with Conrad Smith and his sister, Cecilia— I mean, she really likes his folks and all. They were real nice to us that time we went bowling."

"Oh, well, I guess if it's the Smiths . . . Why don't you put Conrad Senior on the line and I'll just make sure y'all won't be any trouble to 'em."

"Uh, no sir—Mr. Smith—he's not anywhere in here right now. I believe he's . . . he's out loading up every-thing."

"Oh, well—"

"Please, Daddy, I gotta go. They're really in a hurry to get started. It's all right, ain't it?"

"The ten-thirty express to Houston is now ready for immediate—"

See Jimmy clap his hand over the phone. . . .

"Well, all right, son. I'm sure you'll behave yourselves. And I'm trusting you to watch out for your little sister, now, you hear?"

Trusting—oh, man. What an awful word. I came crashing back into my body with a big sick thud. "Yessir," I mumbled. "Thank you, sir."

"Okay then. Y'all have a good time, now."

We said our good-byes then, and I hung up.

"Everything okay?" J.D. asked, as she and Mary Al came hurrying out of the bathroom.

"Yeah, sure," I muttered. I felt like I was gonna throw up, was all.

"You look sorta sick—you want to change your mind? Probably still time to get your money back."

"I'm *fine*," I lied. "You ain't getting rid of me that easy." I grabbed the two elbows again. "If we're going on this dang-fool bus ride, let's *go*."

CHAPTER thirty

The bus driver was a good-size fella with a big round belly and a bushy mustache and the name Blair printed on his pocket. He was standing at the bus door, greeting passengers and taking up tickets.

"Good morning, sir, how are you today? You have a nice trip, now. Watch your step there, ma'am. Can I help you with that bag? Looks like we got another scorcher here, don't we?"

Shoot, I wished we'd got one that didn't pay everybody so durn much attention. And speaking of big bellies, what was old Blair gonna think about J.D.'s? My heart was stuck halfway up my windpipe when her turn came. Was he looking at her funny or was I just imagining it?

"Good morning, young lady." He was smiling, at least. "Visiting friends in Houston?"

"My mom—"

"Her mother—"

"We're going to the zoo," the three of us answered at the same time.

"Oh, well, you've got a nice day for it. Just a little on the hot side for me. But you kids can stand that better than us old folks, can't you?" He peeled a piece off J.D.'s ticket and handed it back to her.

"Yessir," she murmured, climbing aboard.

I was positive he was staring at her coat.

"She's real sensitive to air conditioning," I explained.

"It gives her the hives," said Mary Al.

I shot her a look. The *hives?*

But Blair just nodded like he'd heard it a hundred times before. "Oh," he said, looking after J.D. "Well, I guess it has that effect on some people." He switched his attention to me and Mary Al. "Y'all let me know if you have any problems, now."

"Yessir. We sure will. Thank you, sir."

Lord, I was about making myself sick. Even Conrad Smith never sounded any more like pure cane sugar. But we'd made it on the bus, at least, with nobody any wiser about the Empress.

"In the back," I whispered to J.D., but she was heading for it already.

The bus was only about two-thirds full, so we were able to find three places together in the next-to-last row. J.D. shoved over into the window seat, with me right next to her in case of trouble, and Mary Al sat just across from us on the aisle. There was an old man beside her, who was kind of mumbling to himself, and a mother with a little baby behind him. The pimply-faced soldier from the waiting room had stretched himself out over the two seats behind me, trying to take a nap. None of 'em looked like they were real interested in any of us, thank goodness.

"How's the Empress doing?" I said under my breath, once we all got settled. "She getting nervous yet?"

"I think she's asleep," J.D. whispered back. "She hasn't even moved since we came out of the ladies' room."

"She hasn't?" I'd never known the Empress to go to sleep in broad daylight. Although I guess it didn't look much like daylight to *her*. "Are you sure she's not—"

"No," said J.D., cutting me off. "I can feel her heart beating."

Well, that was good news, at least, I told myself, as the engine revved up and the doors hissed shut and the bus started to move out of the station. I tried to sit back, relax, and leave the driving to Blair, like they say on the commercials, but my conscience was bothering me so bad I couldn't. I kept hearing my daddy say he trusted me, was the problem. Why'd he have to go and say a thing like that?

"Are you sure she's okay?" I asked again after a minute or two. "I mean, maybe you ought to check. Even with this AC on, she's bound to be hot under there."

"Shh," said J.D. "I'll check in a little while. I'm gonna

unbutton the coat and give her some water just as soon as we get on Interstate Ten. By that time everybody'll be staring out the windows."

"What are they gonna be staring out the windows for, J.D.? All you got out there is a bunch of rice fields and chemical plants."

"It'll be okay, Jimmy. Quit worrying so much, will you?"

"Who's worrying? Do I look worried?"

J.D. just rolled her eyes.

I could hear Mary Al and the mumbling man talking together now—something about "Hawaii Five-O." Sounded like they were telling each other their favorite episodes. Mary Al was partial to the one where all the stars had evil twins, but I'm pretty sure the mumbler said he liked it best when they either got hynotized or had amnesia.

Amnesia—wasn't that when a person couldn't remember anything he'd done? I wouldn't have minded a little touch of that myself.

Well, no use bellyaching. It was too late to turn back now. I didn't have me one of them time machines. Best look on the bright side, right? We get to Houston at noon. We hop on one of them city buses that J.D.'s supposed to know so much about and head on over to her mother's place. Then they visit for a little bit, and J.D. calls Mrs. Monroe and tells her she's with her mom now and she's safe and oh by the way the monkey got out and she's real sorry. That ought to put us at about one-thirty. Then either

J.D.'s mom gives us a lift to the zoo or we ride another bus if she's too busy or something, and we take the Empress in and explain her situation and get her signed up for that jungle training course. Ought to be—oh, let's say about three o'clock by then. That leaves us two whole hours to get J.D. to her mom's again and me and Mary Al to the bus station in time for the five o'clock express, which has us back to town and on our bikes and home in time for supper.

And then maybe in twenty years or so I could tell some psychiatrist about it, if it turned out I grew up nuts.

We were pulling out onto the highway now.

"Okay," J.D. whispered. "I'm gonna open up the coat real slow. Just be ready to block me if anybody looks over here or walks by."

I nodded, scared to death. But we didn't have a bit of a problem. The Empress was asleep, all right, wrapped around J.D.'s stomach like a little furry baby. She opened her big eyes and blinked when the sunlight hit her, but she still looked pretty wore out. Just stayed there real sweet and quiet while J.D. fed her the water and a couple grapes.

"See what a good girl she is?" said J.D., looking proud as any mama. She stroked the soft dark spot on the top of the little head. "Don't you worry about a thing, Your Majesty. You're gonna be just fine."

We were both quiet for a good while then. The muscles in my chest actually started to relax a tiny bit. Maybe our luck was gonna hold, after all. Long as Conrad's mother wasn't due at the Cut 'n Curl to get her eyebrows bleached.

"Jimmy?" J.D. was speaking real soft.

"What?"

"How much money you have left over, after that ninety bucks?"

"Why?" I gave her a look. "You need *more*?"

"No. I was just wondering, that's all."

I sighed. "Seven dollars and sixty-nine—no, wait, I spent a quarter on that phone call. . . . Seven dollars and forty-four cents."

"That's it?"

"Yeah, so what?"

She didn't answer right away. She was scratching the Empress behind the ears. "You weren't, you know, saving up for anything special, were you?"

"Naw, nothing much." I didn't really want to talk about it. Just gonna make me feel sick again.

"Mary Al said something about the Grand Canyon."

I shrugged. "It's no big deal."

"Well, yeah it is. I saw it once. It's pretty big."

"No, I mean—you know what I mean." I stared out the window. We were passing a scrubby stretch of pine trees now, coming up on some kind of processing plant with squat white holding tanks and tall skinny smokestacks that were belching little plumes of yellow fire.

I dropped my eyes and fiddled with a loose thread hanging off my shirt. "So how big was it, anyway?"

J.D. sighed. "Pretty #%!* big."

The Empress made a soft little chittering sound. When I turned around she was looking at me, blinking them big eyes. I put a finger in her right hand and watched the monkey fingers close around it, all trusting.

Well, what did I care about the durn Grand Canyon? Just some big hole in the ground. Shoot, I couldn't even spell Phoenix. "I'll go some other time, that's all."

J.D. nodded. We rode along quiet a while more.

"Jimmy?"

"What?"

"I'm gonna pay you back, I swear. First chance I—"

She broke off. She was looking at something in the aisle behind me, so I turned around.

The soldier was standing there, staring right at the Empress.

Lord have mercy. J.D. hugged her tight and tried to pull the coat over her. I pretty much just froze.

The soldier leaned over me and held out a cheese puff.

A little brown hand reached out and grabbed it, then disappeared.

The soldier never said a word. Just stood there a few seconds longer, looking amazed. And then he gave us a wink and went back to his stretched-out seats and pulled his soldier hat over his eyes.

"Aw, man," I muttered, when I could breathe again. "We're never gonna make it."

"Sure we will," said J.D. "Calm down, we're almost there. Look, you can see downtown Houston already."

I looked. Sure enough, there it was—all them fine tall buildings shining in the sun. Kind of took me by surprise, like it always does, rising up so sharp and new-looking out of that flat place. I swear, it was just like we were in Oz or something, on our way to the Emerald City.

Well, except it wasn't green. And I doubted there was a wizard waiting for us. And our monkey hadn't sprouted wings yet, that I could see—

"Jimmy?"

"What?"

"I was just thinking, when we get to Houston—I mean later, when I'm back at my mom's and all—maybe you could come over sometime. We could go check on the Empress, you know, find out how much she's learned."

"Yeah," I said. "Maybe so."

She peeked under the coat, then held it open a little for me to see. The Empress was sleeping again.

J.D. stroked the goldy brown back, real soft and slow. "They're gonna be crazy about her. She'll be the head of her class. 'The most intelligent of all the New World monkeys,' remember?"

I nodded. "Sure, I remember." Sort of sounded like something on a tombstone, but I didn't mention that.

Houston was getting closer now. J.D. started buttoning the coat. "Stop worrying, James Henry. They know me in this town. Everything's gonna be fine, you'll see."

CHAPTER thirty-one

Our first half hour in Houston went right according to schedule. You never saw thirty minutes tick away so tidy. Blair pulled us into the station and opened up the door and thanked us for riding with him and we climbed on out and let J.D. lead the way from there.

She seemed awful proud to be back in her hometown and that it was so big and noisy and crowded and all. Everybody was rushing around like they had someplace real important to go. And hot? Lord. I guess it's all that concrete or something—they have it just about everywhere you look. When J.D. took us outside to the metro stop, there was all kinds of people standing around sweating. I was scared at first that somebody was bound to ask J.D. why she was wearing that fool coat, but no one paid us a bit of mind. They were all too busy fanning theirselves and staring into space.

"How much they charge to ride the bus in Houston?" I asked, counting my seven forty-four for the millionth time.

"Just a quarter for kids under twelve," said J.D. "Don't worry, Jim, we got plenty. I still have nearly ten bucks, remember? No—eleven, thanks to that nice lady."

I groaned. "Don't remind me."

But J.D. was grinning. "Aw, Jimbo, just think how good that made her feel. She won't have to go to church for a month. Anyway, we can always use the cash."

"You think we have enough to buy a hot dog at the zoo?" Mary Al asked. "I'm getting kind of hungry."

"They charge too much at those snack bars," said J.D. "I'll fix us some sandwiches when we get to my place. Look, here comes our bus right now—"

I couldn't help but be impressed that she was so sure which one it was, what with there being so many to choose from and the traffic making so much noise and it being so hot and all. But we just hopped on and paid our quarters and sat down and rode along being grateful for air conditioning, and before we'd hardly even got cooled off good she was saying this was our stop coming up.

Well, we hopped off again then and followed her along a kind of cracked sidewalk on a busy street for a block or so, past a whole lot of little businesses and some filling stations and a Mexican restaurant that smelled real good, and then we turned off from there and got into a more regular neighborhood. J.D. never said anything all this time, but you could tell she was getting pretty excited about being so close to home, because she was walking faster every minute. I followed along with Mary Al, trying to guess which one of these houses was hers. They were kind of old, mostly, but a good many had been fixed up real nice, and I figured with the Monroe money hers would be the nicest of all.

But she didn't stop at any of 'em. We got to the end of that block and durned if she didn't turn down *another* street. The houses here weren't so nice as them others— seemed like every other one had peeling paint and burglar bars. But J.D. didn't turn in any of those, either. She kept on going, faster and faster, until finally the street come to a dead end and there wasn't any place left to go but some crummy old apartments.

For a minute I thought she must've taken a wrong turn somewhere. No kin of Luly Kate Meadowsweet Monroe would ever live *here*. It was one of them places you can't see anybody staying in for very long. Not much to it, really—just two cardboardy-looking stories put together in a plain box shape, with a couple of them big depressing rubber trees leaning against the side wall, and all of it setting there in a pool of grayish gravel.

Even Mary Al knew there was something wrong. She shot me a look—*This ain't it, is it?* But J.D. never held back for a minute. I don't know why she hadn't fainted yet in that heat, with that big coat on and her own private fur wrapper underneath, but she was going even *faster,* if anything. She led us right up the gravel drive and past the dark hole of a parking garage and around one of them smelly Dumpsters with garbage spilling out, then straight up the metal stairs that clanged under our feet and landed us on the second floor.

"Have y'all lived here long?" I asked, trying to make it sound just regular, while J.D. stopped in front of number 204 and fished a key out of her pocket.

She shrugged. "Not too long. Only about six months, I guess." She stuck the key in the lock. "This is just temporary while we're looking around. My mom gets tired of staying in the same old—"

She broke off there. The key wasn't working. "Well, that's weird," she said, trying it again. "Maybe I bent it somehow. . . . Mom?" she called, knocking on the door. "Mom? Are you there? It's me, I'm home—"

No answer.

"Aw, man," I muttered. "I knew we should've called first—"

"Maybe she went to the store," said Mary Al.

"No," said J.D. "She's here, I know she is. She's probably just taking a nap." She banged louder. "Mom? You asleep? Wake up, Mom, it's me!"

Still nothing—from number 204, that is. But the lump under J.D.'s coat was starting to move around and make little yeeping noises.

"J.D.—"

But she was too busy knocking to notice me. "*Mom*— wake up, Mom—it's J.D.!"

Yeep yeep yeep . . .

"*J.D.,*" I said again, shaking her arm this time. "J.D., you're scaring the Empress."

She heard me then. She stopped knocking and started unbuttoning the coat. "Oh, shoot, how long has it been now? She was being so good I'd almost forgot she was there. . . . You okay, Your Majesty? I'm sorry I woke you up—"

The Empress came out then, blinking and dazed-looking, too limp to do much but stare at us and chitter just a little. Like, *Hey, guys, nice to see you again, is the AC broke around here or what?*

"You'd better give her some water, J.D. You have any of them grapes left?"

"Sure," she said. "I think so. We might as well wait here, anyway. My mom'll probably be home in a minute or two."

We all sat down then, best as we could on that narrow slab of concrete, while J.D. took off the coat and checked the pockets. She brought out what was left of the water and a few mashed grapes and a box of raisins.

"If the Empress don't want those, maybe we could split 'em," said Mary Al, looking kind of hopeful.

Not that I blamed her. Pitiful as they were, my stomach was growling at the sight of 'em, itself.

"Maybe we ought to walk back to that Mexican restaurant we passed and pick up a taco or something," I said, looking at my watch. "It's nearly one-thirty already."

"Or else we could go on to the zoo right now," said J.D., "and then I could come back here, and you two could go straight on to the bus station. I'm sure my mom'll be back by—"

"J.D.?" said a kid's voice, right behind me. "Is that your monkey?"

I turned around and saw him then—a chubby little boy with huge blue eyes and curly black hair. He looked like he was maybe three or four, kind of on the runny-nosed side, also barefooted and bare-bellied, except for his Cookie Monster swimming trunks. The door to number 205 was standing open behind him.

"Hey, Hector." J.D. looked up and grinned. "How you been, bud?"

"Can I pet that monkey, J.D.?"

"In a minute, maybe. She's having her lunch right now. Listen, Hector—have you seen my mom? You didn't notice her go out or anything, did you?"

Hector shook his head. "Can I feed the monkey her lunch, J.D.? Please can I feed her?"

"Not yet, Hector, she's not feeling too good. Listen to me, now—think real hard—have you seen my mom at all today?"

Hector wrinkled up his forehead and scratched his ear. "You mean Clarice?"

J.D. sighed. "Yes, Hector, Clarice. My mom—the lady who lives right here. Have you seen her today?"

He shook his head again. And then he smiled. "I

remember Clarice. She used to give me M&M's. She said I could have all the green ones. I like the green ones. When's she coming back, J.D.?"

"I don't *know,* Hector, that's what I'm trying to—"

J.D. broke off there. She went real still. "What do you mean, when's she coming back? Where is she?"

Hector shrugged. "Gone," he said.

You could almost hear the sound of some huge invisible clock busting into a trillion tiny pieces.

Mary Al looked at me. I looked at J.D. J.D. was still sitting there frozen, looking at Hector. "Gone?" she repeated.

Hector nodded and squatted beside us, breathing Frito breath all over the Empress. "Can I pet the monkey now, J.D.?"

J.D. wasn't listening. She stood up and handed the Empress to Mary Al. "Wait here," she said. "I'll be right back. Is your mom home, Hector?" She was already knocking on his door. "Gladys, are you in there? Gladys, it's me—" And then she disappeared inside the apartment without waiting for an answer.

Aw, man . . .

"Jimmy?" Mary Al's eyes were so round, they'da looked right at home in the display case at Dunkin' Donuts. "What do we do now?"

"I don't know." I shook my head. "Wait and see, I guess."

So we waited, and Hector petted the Empress, and

I tried to listen for what was going on next door, and I was glad I hadn't eaten anything now because I'da thrown up for sure. After a while I could hear the sound of voices rising and falling, but I couldn't make out what they were saying, and I was getting so worried that I was just about to go on in there and check on J.D.—

When all of a sudden she's tearing back out of the apartment.

"Come on," she muttered to me and Mary Al. "Go inside, Hector, your mama's looking for you."

"But I wanna pet the monkey—"

"Go inside, Hector!"

Hector opened his eyes wide and went.

"Where are we going?" I asked.

J.D. didn't answer. She was gathering up stuff and starting to put the coat back on.

"J.D.? What's going on?"

She looked at me now. Then she nodded. "Right," she said, taking off the coat again. "You'd better carry her this time. I can't take her with me in there, and Mary Al's too little." She started to put the coat on me.

"J.D.!" I shoved it away. "Answer me, or I ain't doing anything. It's nearly a quarter of two. What's our plan?"

The wolf eyes glared at me. "I don't care what you do. I'm going to get my mother."

CHAPTER thirty-two

It was a quarter *after* two by the time we got back to another bus stop on that same busy street and hopped on a bus that said South Main. I was so thankful to be cool for a minute I almost forgot to worry about everything else. I'd thought I was hot before, but that weren't nothing to what it was now, with the coat on and the furball wrapped around my stomach. And if *I* was hot, I couldn't even hardly imagine how the Empress must be feeling.

"How'd you stand it all this time?" I asked J.D. "I'm about fainting under here already."

She just shrugged and kept staring out the window.

I looked at my watch. Two-twenty-nine. I wondered how much further we had to go. We were coming up on a part of town I remembered now from the times I'd come over here with Mama and Daddy. There was that big white fountain with the traffic going all around it, and the statue of General Sam Houston setting up on his horse, and right behind him that big green park stretching out real pretty—

"Well, that's Hermann Park right there, J.D.—ain't the zoo just on the other side? You decide to go there first after all?"

She shook her head. "I gotta go a couple of stops down," she said. "But y'all might as well get off here. I'll meet you at the main gate in half an hour."

"No way," I said. "We come this far, we're sticking together."

So we rode on past the general and the park and all, and a lot of people got off, and some got on, and in just a few minutes we come up on a whole slew of hospitals and whatnot and signs all over saying Medical Center.

J.D. stood up. "This is it."

My stomach turned over. Wasn't this where people come to get their hearts transplanted and their cancer cured? Oh, Lord, I knew it wasn't no ocean cruise. But I didn't say anything, just nodded and held onto my lumpy belly and grabbed Mary Al's hand and followed J.D. off the bus, and we walked down one sidewalk and turned right on another, and stopped in front of a big pink building.

NEW DAY REHABILITATION AND RECOVERY CENTER, said the sign.

I wasn't sure what that meant, but it didn't sound good.

"Y'all better wait out here," she said. "I'll be right back."

I shook my head. "I told you, we stick together."

"Come *on*, Jimmy. I've gotta talk to my mom. You can't come in here in that coat."

"Well, it wasn't *my* idea to wear the stupid coat—"

"Shh. Five minutes. I'll be right back."

She walked off then, and I tried to tell myself it was okay. I mean, how far could she get?

But half a minute later I got to worrying so bad that I grabbed Mary Al again and we followed her in.

It seemed like a real fine place and all—I mean, for a hospital or whatever it was. The lobby was near as nice as the Howard Johnson back home. I felt pretty silly in the coat, even with the AC blasting, but at least the Empress was sleeping again, and nobody seemed to be looking our way.

"There she is," said Mary Al, pointing across the room to where J.D. was just now stepping inside an elevator. So we hauled it over there and jumped in with her, a split second before the doors slid shut.

Well, she glared at us and all, but she couldn't say anything, since there were three or four other people in there with us. But as soon as we stepped out on the fifth floor, she let me have it.

"What do you think you're doing? I told you to wait—"

"It was too hot out there, okay? The Empress would've melted. Anyhow, we ain't gonna bother you one—"

"Can I help you children?"

We all three turned around and found a tall lady looking at us. She had one of them stethoscopes hanging around her neck.

J.D. shot me a *Shut up and let me do the talking* look,

which I was only too happy to do. "Uh, yes, ma'am," she said. "I was just looking for my mother's room—Clarice Monroe? They said downstairs she'd be in five thirteen."

The tall lady smiled. "You must be J.D. We were talking about you just this morning."

You never saw a face go so red so quick. But J.D. managed a nod, at least.

"And these are—friends of yours?"

J.D. looked at me for a second. "Yes, ma'am," she muttered.

The tall lady thought that over. I held my breath. Under the overcoat, I could feel the monkey's heart beating, slow and steady. "Well, the rules say immediate family, but I guess as long as you're quiet—" She checked her watch. "It's nearly three. Why don't you try the common room first? Straight down this hall—the double doors on your right."

I started breathing again.

The common room was a big bright place, with ten or twelve people in it—some in robes and slippers, like you'd expect, but most of 'em dressed in just regular clothes. There was one group watching TV and a few ladies sitting at a card table and an old guy playing Ping-Pong with a teenage girl. The green eyes swept over 'em in a second—no and no and no. "She must be in her room," said J.D. "We might as well—"

She broke off there. She had seen someone, after all. So I looked where she was looking—

A blond-headed lady was sitting off by herself in a big chair by a sunny window, thumbing through a magazine. Even from this far off, you could tell she was pretty. She was kind of thin, I guess, and sort of tired and lonesome-looking, but she didn't seem sick or anything. She wasn't wearing one of them hospital gowns, just jeans and a sweatshirt.

She didn't see us come in, but J.D. sure saw her.

"Is that your mom?" asked Mary Al.

J.D. didn't answer. Seemed like she'd forgot all about us. Never said a word, only took a deep breath and started walking over there as quick as she could.

Mary Al was about to follow her, but I grabbed her shoulder. "They ain't seen one another all summer. They don't need us butting in."

J.D. was clear across the room now, she was almost there, she was standing in front of her mother's chair, saying something. And now Clarice was looking up at her, like she couldn't believe her own eyes. She was on her feet, she was hugging J.D. real hard.

"Come on, Mary Al." I pulled her over to a couch nobody was using. "Let's just wait over here till she calls us. . . ."

I tried not to stare or anything. I knew it was none of my business. I found us some old *National Geographics* and handed one to Mary Al. But I never read a word, and my eyes wouldn't stay on the pictures. They kept wandering over to J.D. and her mom.

They weren't saying much at first, just hugging one another and smiling, and the mom kept touching J.D.'s face like she couldn't get over it. And then she pulled a chair close to hers, and they both sat down, and finally J.D. started talking—just a little at a time, like she was asking questions. So then her mother would answer, and J.D. would ask another one, and it looked like her mother was trying real hard to explain something. But J.D. didn't want to hear it, whatever it was—she was talking again, talking faster now. And for a while her mom listened, but then she started shaking her head—slow at first, and then harder and harder. I could see her trying to get a word in edgewise—*no* was all she wanted to say—but J.D. wouldn't let her, she wouldn't stop talking, she was going a mile a minute now. And finally she got up out of her chair and begun tugging on her mother's arm, like she was trying to make her get up, too. But her mom just kept sitting there, shaking her head no, until J.D. couldn't stand it any more. She knelt on the floor and put her arms around that thin waist and buried her head in her mother's lap.

Mary Al looked at me. "Is it time to go over there?" she asked. But if it hadn't been our business before, it sure as heck wasn't now. The mom was petting J.D.'s hair and talking real easy to her, trying to explain her side, I guess, and calm her down some. And this went on for a good while, until finally J.D. was pretty much quieted. I saw her look up then, and ask her mother one more question, but Clarice just touched J.D.'s face again and shook her head, *no*.

J.D. went real still. The way she had in the bus station when I said I wouldn't give her the six bucks. And then she stood up and turned around and started walking away, walking back toward the double doors, walking faster and faster until she was almost running. So her mom stood up and called to her. "Joy!" I heard her say, "please—you don't understand—" But J.D. wasn't listening, she was out the doors and nearly to the elevator, and me and Mary Al were following just as quick as we could. And I looked over my shoulder and saw the mom starting to come after us, but the tall lady was with her now, she was talking to her, trying to hold her back.

"J.D.—wait," I said.

"For what?" The elevator doors slid open.

"For your mother—she's calling you—"

Only just then the lump under my coat started squirming, and them weak little *yeeping* sounds come out, and now the mom and the tall lady were both walking in our direction—

So I grabbed my stomach like I had the bellyache and jumped on the elevator with J.D. and pulled Mary Al in with us just as the doors slid closed.

CHAPTER thirty-three

There wasn't any time to talk about what had happened. Even if J.D. had been in a talking mood—which she wasn't—we wouldn'tta had the breath for it. We tore out of that New Day place like it was burning down behind us and hit the pavement running, stopping just long enough on the next corner to give the Empress a little air.

"I'll take her now," J.D. muttered. She wouldn't look at me or anything, only gathered up the poor limp lump and hugged her tight.

"Is she okay?" asked Mary Al. "She's breathing kind of funny—"

J.D. shook her head real fierce. "No, she's not—"

"This coat's gonna kill her." I started taking it off. "It's awful hot, J.D.—"

J.D. thought that over quick. Then she nodded. "Okay, chuck it." Sounded like she was gritting her teeth. "No sense waiting for any more buses. We can walk from here."

Wasn't gonna be any walking to it, though. I pitched the poor old coat in the nearest trash can and we took off running again, J.D. hanging onto that monkey like a little furry football. Charging along the sidewalk, zigzagging around surprised-looking people—folks in wheelchairs and a lady on crutches and a daddy pushing his twin toddlers in one of them double strollers.

"Monkey!" the closest kid hollered as we raced past, but we never stopped, just kept running and running, back past all them big hospitals and across two or three busy streets and then veering off through the park when we come to it, with J.D. and the Empress out in front and me dragging Mary Al along. And pretty soon we were past the swings and seesaws and swirly slides and coming up on the duck lake and that old-timey train, and the zoo was just another fifty yards or so ahead—

When all of a sudden I remembered about J.D.'s grandma. She never had called her, had she? Well, shoot, she was in for it now. . . . But then what would she have told her, anyway? She couldn't stay here with her mom in that—whatever that place was. She'd have to go back with us, that's all. Maybe we could say the Smiths had invited her, too. . . .

But there wasn't any time to think about it now. Already my watch said four-oh-four. That gave us exactly fifty-six minutes to drop off the Empress and get her all squared away and still make it back to the big bus station for that five o'clock express. Thank the Lord I got them three round trips, I said to myself, as we crossed one last street and come barreling up to the zoo ticket booth.

"Three kids," I panted.

"A dollar fifty," said a tinny little microphone voice. The man behind the window looked like he was half-asleep.

I shoved the money in the metal tray. "Thank you, sir," I said, and we started to walk away.

But then I took a look at the map he had give me, and I could see it wasn't gonna be nearly enough. So I told J.D. and Mary Al to hold on a minute, and I headed on back to the window.

"Excuse me," I said. "Could you show me on this map where they train the monkeys?"

The man's eyes were still half-shut. "Monkeys straight back past the sea lions and the aviary, just opposite the main concession stands."

"No sir, we ain't looking for the locked-up monkeys. I seen them before. What we need is the training offices."

"Training offices?"

"You know, where the scientists work. We're trying to get our monkey set up with them jungle classes."

"Get your *what*?" All of a sudden the man looked wide awake.

"Our monkey," said J.D., holding the Empress up for him to see.

But the man looked all upset, for some reason. The

microphone squeaked. "You can't take that animal in the zoo. It's against the rules."

I just stared at him. The poor fella was nuts, that was all there was to it. "Y'all don't allow animals in the *zoo?*"

"Well, yes—I mean, no—only *wild* animals," the man sputtered. "No *pets* allowed, is what I'm saying."

"No sir," I tried to explain. "This ain't like our regular pet—"

"We want to get her trained up for the jungle," added Mary Al.

"Trained up?" said the man. "I'm sorry, I don't know what you're talking about—"

"For the *jungle,*" Mary Al said real loud, like he was hard of hearing.

"I'm *sorry,*" said the mechanical voice. "No pets allowed."

There was a little crowd gathering around us now, staring and pointing and whispering. A kid tried to pet the Empress, but his mother jerked his hand away.

I looked at my watch again: four-oh-nine. This guy was killing us. "Maybe you could call your boss," I said. "We're running real late already—"

But the man in the box kept shaking his head. "My boss knows the rules same as me. I told you already, no pets."

J.D. was getting madder by the minute. "Why do you keep calling her a pet? She's a *monkey,* for crying out loud.

This is a *zoo,* don't you get it? What are you, some kind of—"

"*Please,* sir," I interrupted. "It's kind of an emergency. If you could just please call somebody—"

But the tin man wouldn't stop shaking his head and we couldn't sneak in since we'd chucked the durn coat and now my watch said four-eleven—

"What's the trouble here, Leonard?" said a voice just behind me. "Anything I can do?"

I turned around and saw a nice-looking gray-headed man standing there, holding his little grandson's hand. He had a Friends of the Zoo tag pinned to his shirt.

"Oh, hello, Buddy," said Leonard. "I didn't see you back there. These kids don't understand the rules, that's all."

The gray-headed man nodded. "I couldn't help over-hearing. I tell you what, why don't you give Dr. Goodsell a call? She'll know how to help these youngsters."

"Well, I imagine she's busy, Buddy. No sense bothering her. The rules are real clear—"

"It's okay, Leonard. I'll take responsibility. Timothy and I were planning to stop by and see her, anyway. You just give her a buzz, why don't you? Say we'll meet her in her office in five minutes."

Leonard thought this over for a while. His window was getting all steamed up, he was worrying so hard. Finally he heaved a big sigh and picked up the phone. "Well, all right then, Buddy. Seeing as how it's you. But I'm washing my hands of the whole deal, you hear?"

CHAPTER thirty-four

"Thank you, sir," I said, as we walked on through the gate.

"Don't mention, it, son," said Buddy. "You just caught Leonard on one of his strict days, that's all. . . . Hey, there, Miss Annie! Nice to see you again. These children are all with me. How are you, Elizabeth? Tell K.K. I said hello. . . . Have those egret eggs hatched yet, Jeffrey?"

Seemed like he knew everybody in the place—the girl selling popcorn and the redheaded security guard and the guy cleaning out the sea lion pool. All of 'em just smiled and waved back, once they seen it was Buddy, and never worried us at all. It was almost like having one of them guardian angels, like you see on TV.

Only problem was, with so many friends to speak to, and Buddy asking us questions about the Empress, seemed like it took forever to get where we were going—past the birds and the reptile house and that dark place where they keep the bats and all them big-eyed night creepers. It gave me that peculiar feeling in my stomach, like it always does. I mean, I like the zoo and all—when I was little it was my favorite place in the whole world. But then I started having this dream—it was *me* in one of them cages, and I couldn't get out. I'd try to tell 'em I was a human, but they couldn't hear me, and I'd wake up sweating, and now it seems like I never can go over there without thinking of that.

Anyway, we kept on walking, and after a while we passed a whole big batch of monkeys looked kind of like the Empress, and they got all excited when we tried to show 'em to her, but she was too limp to care much. And then we went on back past the lions and tigers and fake gorilla mountain and over into the children's zoo, and my watch was closing in on four-twenty before Buddy knocked on a door marked EMILY G. GOODSELL, D.V.M.

"Hey, Doc!" he said, when a smiling lady in a white coat opened it. "Just making sure you aren't dozing off back here."

"Hello, Buddy," said the doctor. "What kind of trouble you stirring up today?"

Well, then they shook hands like old friends, and she visited with the grandson awhile, and then Buddy explained a little about us and took Timothy off to pet the llamas.

"So," said the doctor. She turned to J.D., who was hugging the Empress tighter than ever. "Is this your monkey?"

"My dad gave her to me," said J.D. Her voice had that fierce sound to it again.

"I see." The doctor waited. "May I have a look?"

For a second there, I thought J.D. had changed her mind about the whole thing. After coming all this way and having all this trouble, looked as if she just couldn't stand to give her up. But the doctor seemed like somebody you could trust, and we were running out of time real bad now—

"Go on, J.D.," I said. "It's what we come for, remember? This doctor wouldn't hurt her, would you, ma'am?"

Dr. Goodsell shook her head. "Not for the world."

J.D. thought about it a couple more seconds. Then she touched the little furry head one last time and handed her over. "Her name's the Empress."

The doctor smiled. "Royalty, hmm?" She carried her over to an examining table. "Let's get you checked out, then, Your Highness." She looked at J.D. again. "Did you bring her records with you?"

J.D. went pale. "Records?"

"Her medical records. It would help if I knew a little of her history."

"I—I forgot 'em. But I know all about her—"

"Well, maybe you can answer some of my questions, then. Was she bred in captivity?"

Mary Al's eyes went wide. "What kind of bread?" You could just hear her wondering, thin-sliced or butter-top.

"She means was she born in a cage," I said.

J.D. nodded. "On a pet ranch out I-45. She's about four years old. . . . She loves grapes. . . . She's a capuchin. . . ."

"Right," said the doctor. "They're marvelous, aren't they? Such wonderful little hands—"

"Yes, ma'am," I said. "She's real smart—" and then we were all talking at once.

"The most intelligent of all the New World monkeys—"

"We got her half-trained already—"

"She outsmarts squirrels most every day—"

"She hardly ever comes out of the trees anymore, so the tigers couldn't get her—"

"And she knows how to catch stuff—"

"She eats lizards—"

"And berries—"

"And frogs—"

"So we figured—"

"She'd really do great—"

"In one of y'all's classes—"

"Classes?" Dr. Goodsell looked confused. "What classes?"

Well, my stomach sunk down some when she said that. But I told myself we just weren't explaining it right. So then we went through the whole thing—how we'd seen it on television, about the endangered monkeys, and how we'd been taking her over to the island but now we couldn't, and how she'd been so sad she'd made herself sick, and we knew she'd be so much happier in the Amazon. And Dr. Goodsell listened to every bit of it while she checked out the Empress, real gentle, and she nodded like she was understanding—

But when we finally paused for breath, and she was done with her examining, she looked at us standing all around her and shook her head.

"I'm so sorry," she said. "I can see how much you want to help. And what you saw on television—it's real, it's really being done. But I'm afraid there's no program like that for capuchins. They're not endangered."

Dead silence. For a good ten seconds, we all just stared at one another. And then J.D. busted out of it—

"What do you mean, not endangered? *She's* endangered—just look at her!"

"She'll die in that cage!" said Mary Al.

Dr. Goodsell sighed. She took a pear out of her pocket and handed it to the Empress, who took a half-hearted bite and then let it drop. "You don't understand. The programs you're talking about—returning these creatures to the wild—they're enormously difficult and expensive. It can't be done for *every* animal. I wish it could. But there's no way, so they've had to choose—it's not just individuals they're trying to save, but the whole species. And capuchins are thriving; they're in no danger of dying out. They're so adaptable, they can live almost anywhere."

Remarkably prolific, highly adaptable, common in Central and South American rain forests from Honduras to Paraguay . . .

"You mean being smart ain't in their *favor*?" I asked.

"But that ain't *fair*!" said Mary Al.

"What's fair got to do with it?" J.D. was starting to look dangerous again. "You mean there's already plenty of 'em, right? So what does one matter, more or less?"

"No," said the doctor. "I know it sounds harsh—that's not what I'm saying—"

"Yes, ma'am, it is." My stomach was hurting. "No sense calling a mule a music teacher."

"Excuse me?"

I took a deep breath and blew it out. From far away I could hear the locked-up lions roaring. An elephant made one of them trumpet noises—*aauuuaaahh!* "Ain't there anything you can do for her?" I asked.

"Have you thought about—" the doctor began.

But before she could finish answering me, there was a knock on the door. "Excuse me just a minute," she said. "I'll be right back."

She went to the door then, and stood there talking to somebody, while me and Mary Al and J.D. looked at one another.

"What do we do now?" asked Mary Al.

"Nothing we *can* do," I said. "We go home, that's all." I checked my watch. Good Lord—it was four-thirty-four! "We gotta go right now—that express leaves in less than half an hour—"

J.D. picked up the Empress. "Y'all go on," she said. "I'm not going back."

"What are you talking about? You don't have any choice, J.D. Your mom—"

"That's just temporary, okay? I've got friends here. I can stay with Gladys and Hector till she comes home."

"No way, J.D. I ain't leaving you with Hector—"

"What are you gonna do about it? Drag me to the bus station?"

"I will if I have to—"

"No, you won't. I'm not going, and neither is the Empress. She can't—the coat's gone, remember? And I'm not leaving her here, not now."

Oh, brother, that stupid coat! We'd never get her on the bus without it! "Well, come on—we'll just have to run back and get it out of that trash can—we can catch the bus from there—"

"Forget it, Jimmy. We'd never make it. There's not enough time. Y'all just go on. I'll figure something out."

"*No.* I ain't leaving here without you, J.D.—"

"Joy Dolores Monroe?"

We all froze. That redheaded security guard was standing inside the door beside Dr. Goodsell.

"Are you Joy Monroe?" he asked again.

J.D. just stared at him. How did this guy know her name? We hadn't told anybody who we were, not even the doctor. . . .

He was looking at me and Mary Al now. "James Harbert? Mary Alice Harbert?"

Lord have mercy. . . .

"And is that the animal belonging to Mrs. Luly Kate Monroe?"

"Well, sort of—"

"Not exactly—"

"Nobody *owns* her," J.D. snarled.

"I'm gonna have to ask you kids to come with me."

CHAPTER thirty-five

Mary Al looked at me. I looked at J.D. J.D. held on to the Empress and said, "Run!"

It wasn't smart, I know. Smart didn't have anything to do with it. Any more'n it does in one of them nightmares when they're after you. We just had to get out of there, was all, and maybe still make that bus. Wasn't any time to think it over, anyhow. J.D. was already out the door— not the one being blocked by the doctor and the red-headed guy, but the one just behind us that led who knew where. So I grabbed Mary Al by the hand and we went running after her, and next thing I know we're charging through some kind of animal nursery and there's baby birds peeping and somebody feeding a baby leopard a bottle and a whole batch of baby foxes scuffling around in their cage, and then a bunch of people hollering all at once:

"Hey! You kids aren't allowed back here!"

"Look—she's got a monkey—"

"What monkey?"

"They're stealing a baby monkey—"

"Somebody stop those kids—"

"Quick! Lock all the doors—"

But we're quicker'n they are—before they even understand what's going on, J.D.'s found a door that opens to some kind of walk-through place, where about a thousand little kids are sticking their noses up against the windows, looking at baby chickens. So we plow our way through 'em and run out of there, and for about half a second I'm thinking we got away—

But then a terrible loud whistle blows somewhere behind us, and I look over my shoulder and see the red-headed guy, and he's coming for us and hollering, "Somebody stop those kids!"

So we just keep running—past the petting place and the aqua-tunnel and straight through the prairie dog town, where all them little critters click at us and go diving down their holes, and then we jump that short wall and keep on going, right past the baby elephant and out the kiddie gate. And when I look over my shoulder the redhead is *still* coming, and now it looks like he's speaking into his walkie-talkie. . . .

"We gotta split up!" J.D. hollers. "He can't follow all three of us at once—"

"No!" I holler back. "We stick together!"

"Don't be a jerk, Jimmy! Y'all go back by the camels— I'll take the bears. Meet you at the main gate in five minutes—"

"No!" I holler again. But she's faster'n the two of us,

is the thing. We try to keep up, but we can't—I can see her up ahead of us, now, turning into that long bear row. So we follow her past all them big trenches and fake caves, where the polar bears and Kodiaks and grizzlies are all dead asleep in the heat, and then she's turning left and heading over toward the snow leopard—

When all of sudden I spot another security guard coming at her from behind the crocodile pond.

"J.D.!" I holler. "Watch out!"

She sees him then and turns back our way, but the redheaded guard is still behind us, so she veers right over by the monkeys. And I guess they get wind of the Empress, because they're all screaming and screeching and bouncing off their branches, and Mary Al is starting to drag—she's skinned her knee somehow. And now here's a third guy coming from who knows where, and we're all zigging and zagging every whichaway, and there's whistles blowing and mothers fussing and monkeys screeching and people hollering and kids crying and losing their balloons—

So J.D. turns one way, and then another, and another, and then she's swinging around and heading back toward us again. But the redhead is right behind us now, and just as the second guy gets ahold of her arm, hands grab me by the shoulders and a voice says, "Gotcha!"

They didn't take us to jail or anything. Though I doubt we could've felt much worse if they had. It was just a plain old room in the security building, a little bigger'n closet size. Looked like one of them places you sit in at your dentist's office while you're waiting for him to get around to drilling your teeth. It had a love seat and a couple chairs and a vase of plastic daisies on the coffee table, and even some magazines piled up there for our reading pleasure: *American Real Estate—The Christmas Bonus Issue* and *Outdoor Lighting and Living* and *Security Today, Your Law Enforcement Quarterly*.

They never yelled at us at all, or even talked to us that much—well, not after J.D. bit the redhead when he took the Empress from her. She wouldn't answer any of their questions, anyway. Not that it mattered. They already knew everything about us, somehow. They just took our pictures and filled out some forms and said the six most awful words in the English language: "Your parents are on their way."

It was the redhead who put us in the room. He wasn't much more'n a kid himself. He was holding the Empress with one hand and pressing a wad of Kleenex on his bitten wrist. I don't think J.D. had actually broke the skin or anything, but I felt sort of bad for him, anyway. He seemed like a pretty nice fella, just doing his job.

"Y'all can wait in here till they come," he said, and then he closed us in, and we could hear the sound of the door being locked from the other side.

Good God Almighty.

"But how did they *find* us?" Mary Al wailed. "How did they *know*?"

I just shook my head. It didn't matter how. They knew, that was all. They always knew. I should've known they would. Seemed like I never done anything wrong my whole life without them knowing. That time I spilled that whole bottle of quick-dry glue on the new couch? Took 'em about five minutes to notice. The day Danny and me accidentally blew up the vacuum cleaner? Twenty-five seconds. But nothing—not even that whole awful mess with the tree house and the boat wreck and getting fired from my very first job—*nothing* I'd done had ever been as bad as this.

"I'm trusting you—" That was what Daddy had said. That's what killed me more'n anything. If I was him, I'd never trust me again.

Mary Al cried herself to sleep after a while, but me and J.D. just sat there for about half an hour, staring any-where but at each other. I couldn't hardly stand to look at her, to tell you the truth. I even picked up that Christmas book and stared at a gingerbread house. But my stomach was so empty that made me feel like I was gonna throw up, so I put it down and stared at my shoes.

Looked like I'd managed to step in tar somewhere along the way.

A little ripping sound made me turn my head.

"What are you doing, J.D.?"

She didn't answer. She was tearing strips of paper from the guard magazine, then wadding them up and planting them around the fake daisies. Doing it real careful, like a big art project or something.

"Quit that, will you?"

She didn't look up. *Rrriipp!* went the paper.

"Quit it, J.D.—"

Rrrriiippppp!

I jerked the fool magazine out of her hands. "I said *quit it*, you crazy girl. Ain't we in enough trouble already?"

She looked at me now. That durn kicked-kid look again—so mad and full of hurt it stopped my breath. And then she shrugged and turned away. "You should have gone to the #$%!@ Grand Canyon."

"No kidding," I muttered.

"Yeah, well, nobody asked you to come to Houston, did they?"

There wasn't any answer for that. I gritted my teeth and shut up again.

Mary Al snored a little—one of them jerky after-sob deals.

I stared at my watch. Six-eighteen. An hour and a half to drive. . . If they left at five-thirty, they'd be getting here in forty-two minutes.

Forty-two minutes.

I wondered would the governor call.

"What do you think they'll do with the Empress?" J.D. asked, real low.

"I don't know," I said. "Give her back to your grandma when she gets here, I guess."

"She won't come, she'll just send Jasper. She never leaves that place. She wouldn't drive all the way here for a monkey she doesn't even care about."

I almost said, *What about for her grandkid?* But then I thought better of it. "Well—maybe they'll keep her here, after all. She looked pretty bad off, J.D. That doctor was real nice—I bet she'd help her."

J.D. shook her head. "That's what being smart'll get you. Stuck in a cage with all your little smart friends."

"At least she'd *have* friends. That's better'n not having 'em."

She didn't say anything to that. Another minute crawled by.

"So how much trouble will you be in?" she asked.

I sighed. "I don't know. Plenty."

Another silence. Then:

"I'm sorry."

"Forget it. You were right, nobody asked me to come. I done it on my own."

"Yeah, well . . . I'm sorry, anyway."

"It's okay. They'll get over it. I'll be grounded for a couple years, that's all."

She looked like she would've smiled at that, if she could've.

"What about you?" I asked, after another minute. "How mad will your grandma get?"

She shrugged. "It doesn't matter. I'm not sticking around that place. I got back here once, I can do it again."

I didn't like the sound of that. I thought it over for a minute. "So your mom—you think she'll be coming home pretty soon?"

J.D. didn't answer right away. She looked at me . . . like she was trying to decide something. "I don't know," she said finally. "I thought she was out of there. She *was* out, last time I talked to her. She said she was fine, she said she was never going back." J.D. shook her head. "The old lady must've got to her again."

"Your grandma? What'd she do?"

"She locked her up, that's what she did. In that place— you saw it—"

"But that's a hospital. They don't lock people up."

"It's the same thing. She didn't want to go there, okay? But the old lady made her—I don't know how—she had the lawyers do it. They told some judge my mom was sick—they said she couldn't take care of me. But they got it all wrong—we were doing okay. It wasn't like they made it sound. She just got down sometimes, that's all. After my dad—after the accident—well, anybody would've. And sometimes she couldn't sleep—she'd start worrying about money and everything—"

"Money?" I didn't understand. "But Mrs. Monroe—"

"We didn't want her money. But she wouldn't stop butting in. We kept moving, but she always found us. One time she sent a check, and my mom was so mad, she tore it up. But then she wished she hadn't. She started crying and everything. And that night she couldn't sleep, so she took some pills—"

"Sleeping pills?"

"It was just an accident. She didn't mean to take too many, she just got mixed up. I always watched her so she wouldn't. It was only that one time."

"So what'd you do?"

"I called 911—don't look like that, Jimmy—I told you, it was just an accident. They took her to a regular hospital, that's all. It wasn't that bad. They were gonna let her come home in a couple of days. But old Granny, she found out about it. They said my mom had her number in her purse or something. Next thing I know, she's got her locked up in that place, and they're hauling me off to East Texas."

Aw, man. And I thought *I* had problems. No wonder she'd been so mad, if that was how she saw it. "But J.D., your grandma—she was only trying to help—"

"We didn't *need* her help. I told you, we were doing just fine."

"But your mom—today—she didn't want to leave. Why would she say that, if she didn't mean it?"

J.D. shook her head. "I don't know. They've got her brainwashed or something. She kept saying it was different—she'd gone back on her own this time. She said nobody ever locked her up, she did it herself. A lot of crazy stuff like that—I don't know, it didn't make any sense."

"Sure it does. I mean, if she thinks they're helping her—"

"She doesn't need their help, long as she's got me. It's nobody else's business—she's *my* mom."

"But you're just a kid. You can't do it all by yourself—"

"Sure I can. I did it before. Whose side are you on, anyway?"

"It ain't about sides, J.D. It ain't a *war*."

She didn't answer me. Just sat there all folded up into herself down there at the end of the love seat, with her legs tucked under her and her arms crossed tight and her chin on her chest. She didn't look so big now, without the coat. And no wolf hat, either—she'd given up all her disguises for the Empress, hadn't she? Not that it had done either of 'em any good. And now her magic was gone, she was unprotected, she was just a plain kid again, sitting over there all clenched up like a fist.

"Jimmy?" It was Mary Al, waking up. We'd got kind of loud, I guess.

"What?"

"I'm awful hungry."

I looked at my watch. Six-forty-seven. And we hadn't eaten a bite since breakfast. "I'll ask 'em if they got some crackers or something," I said, and I started to knock on the door—

But just then there was a clicking sound, and it swung open on its own, and the redheaded guy was standing there looking at us. "Time's up, kids," he said, real cheerful. "Your folks are here."

CHAPTER thirty-six

They were standing there waiting for us at the desk in the front office. Looked like they'd dressed up for somebody's funeral. Mama had on her Sunday best, high heels and everything, and Daddy still had on the suit from his Wal-Mart interview. Jasper was wearing his dark chauffeur's uniform and holding his cap. And Mrs. Monroe was there, too—J.D. had been wrong; she'd come out the gate, after all. It was real strange seeing her away from her house, like running into your English teacher at the wrestling matches. Her back was just as straight as ever, but her lipstick was kind of crooked. As if her hand was shaking when she put it on.

You never saw four grimmer-looking faces.

"I'm sorry, Mama," wailed Mary Al, throwing herself in our mother's arms.

"I know, baby," said Mama, hugging her tight.

Daddy just looked at me. "You really done it this time, didn't you, son?"

I hung my head. "Yessir."

Meanwhile Mrs. Monroe hadn't moved. Seemed like she couldn't. "Are you all right, Joy?" she finally managed. "Are all of you all right?"

J.D. didn't answer—she was busy chewing a thumbnail—so I said, "Yes, ma'am, we're all okay."

The redhead cleared his throat. "Uh, Mrs. Monroe?" he said, looking at her. "I'm Chris Martin—I believe I spoke to you on the phone earlier?"

"Yes," said Mrs. Monroe. Seemed like every word was killing her. I guess she hadn't spent much time in correctional facilities. "Thank you for . . . thank you for everything."

"Glad we could help," said Chris. "Now if you folks don't mind, there's some paperwork I'll need for you to fill out. Then you can stop by Dr. Goodsell's office for your monkey, and you're free to go."

"Thank you," Mrs. Monroe said again. "If there's a fine, I'll be glad to—"

"No, ma'am, we're gonna waive all that, considering the age of the perpetra—of the kids. There wasn't any actual damage or anything." Which I thought was real nice of him, considering the little glob of Kleenex still stuck to his arm.

It was past seven by the time we knocked on the doctor's door, but the afternoon sun was still shining, what with daylight savings and all. I wondered if she'd stayed late just for us. "Come in," she said. "I'm glad you're here."

"Where is she?" asked J.D. "Is she gonna be okay?"

"She's resting," said the doctor. "Please, everyone, come in. . . . I'm sorry—I'm Emily Goodsell, we haven't met. . . ."

Well, then the grown-ups had to do all their handshaking and helloing and *We surely do appreciate your trouble*-type talk, and the rest of us stood it as long as we could, and then J.D. busted out again with, "Just tell us what's wrong, will you? Is she gonna die or what?"

The doctor shook her head. She was a real nice lady, but she was looking awful serious now. "I don't think so," she said. "Not as long as she gets the right care. I see no sign of actual disease. But she's exhausted—she was terribly dehydrated when you brought her in. We've been feeding her intravenously for the last hour."

I looked at J.D. "It was that stupid coat."

"Excuse me?" said Dr. Goodsell.

"Nothing. I'm sorry. . . ."

"So what exactly does that mean?" asked Mrs. Monroe. "Does she need to be in an animal hospital? Is there one nearby? Or—is there any way we could leave her with you?"

Dr. Goodsell shook her head again. "I'm afraid I can't treat private pets here. And she really shouldn't be moved right now. But if you can get me her records, and you're willing to donate her to the zoo, we might be able to keep her."

For a minute, nobody breathed. Me and Mary Al and J.D. were frozen, waiting to hear what Mrs. Monroe would say. Finally she nodded. "Well, that sounds reasonable. If you think it can be arranged—"

"No!" J.D. came to life again. "We didn't bring her here just to put her in another cage!"

Mrs. Monroe looked confused. "Then why *did* you bring her here, Joy?"

J.D. wiped her nose. "I thought they could send her back to the rain forest. I thought she could go free. It's not fair, just because she's the wrong type."

"The wrong type?"

"I'm afraid there's been a misunderstanding," said the doctor. "Apparently the children saw a program on TV—" And then she tried to explain, and we tried to explain, and Daddy nodded and said he remembered that show, and pretty soon it sounded like the United Nations or something, everybody speaking different languages and all them machines busted so nobody knew what anybody else was saying:

". . . a very common species . . ."

". . . twice as long in captivity . . ."

". . . but what kind of life is . . ."

". . . how would *you* like it . . ."

". . . got nothing to do with fair . . ."

". . . she'll die in that cage . . ."

The doctor held up her hands for quiet. She looked at Mrs. Monroe. "They were trying to save her life," she said.

"I see." The old lady nodded. Her eyes went to J.D., who was still standing there, all clenched up. "I see. . . ." She turned back to the doctor. "But we don't really have a choice now, do we? Do you have any other suggestions?"

Dr. Goodsell shook her head. "I'm sorry," she said. "I wish I did."

Mrs. Monroe thought this over. Then she nodded one more time and looked at J.D. again. "Joy?" she said.

No answer.

"Joy, you heard the doctor. We don't have a choice. If she's really so unhappy at home—what else can we do?"

J.D. turned away. I saw a fat tear fall on her folded-up arms and roll down to her wrist.

Mrs. Monroe saw it, too. Looked like she wanted to wipe it away, but she didn't know how. She cleared her throat, instead. "Well, then, doctor, if you wouldn't mind making the arrangements—"

They started talking then about what-all had to be done, but right then someone shook my shoulder. I looked around and saw Jasper, who'd been standing back there the whole time, I guess, so quiet I'd forgot all about him. But now he was shaking my shoulder and giving me a scrap of paper with something scribbled on it—he was still holding the pencil in his big hand. *Read it,* he nodded at me.

I read it. There was only five words: *Tell her about the island.*

I just looked at him. What good would that do? We'd been through that already. Wasn't any of my business, anyhow. I shook my head and handed the paper back, but he scribbled something else on it and shoved it at me.

Tell her, he'd written again. *Last chance.*

The words raised the hairs on the back of my neck. Last chance—was that true? Aw, man . . . he was right, wasn't he? There wasn't no time machine gonna fly down here and fix things—tomorrow or last week or next year— wasn't anybody gonna let us come back and do *now* over. It was just gonna tick on by and that big gate would slam shut and I'd probably never see J.D. again—

"Excuse me," I said, pushing over to the desk, where Mrs. Monroe was filling out some form the doctor had given her. "I know it ain't none of my business—" Daddy shot me a warning look, but I figured, what the heck, I was already grounded for the rest of my life. "But Jasper, he just reminded me—there's one thing y'all haven't talked about yet—"

Mrs. Monroe looked up at me. She seemed awful tired. "What's that, James?"

I took a deep breath. "The island."

"The island?" She raised her eyebrows. "I don't under-stand."

"She could live over there—at least part-time, like she done before. Ain't nobody else using it."

Mrs. Monroe shook her head. "That's out of the question."

But I kept on. "It would make her well—I know it would. She was always so happy over there. She wasn't just a common little monkey—she was the Empress. And she got used to being free—that's why she fell sick, when she couldn't go there no more."

"Jim Junior," said Daddy. "You're way out of line here, son—"

"Please, Mrs. Monroe. You wouldn't need a cage or nothing—she could use the tree house when it rained—"

The old lady went real still. Now Mama was shaking her head at me—

"I'm sorry, ma'am," I went on, fast as I could, "I'm real sorry about your boy and everything. But I bet he'd like it—J.D. said he gave the Empress to you so y'all would be friends again. All the rest of it—it never should've happened—"

I run out of breath there. I didn't know what else to say. Mrs. Monroe was so still, I was scared I'd killed her. Put a stake through her heart, like Danny'd said. She looked at me for a minute more. And then she cleared her throat and turned to the doctor.

"Is it possible?" she asked, real quiet. "Could an animal miss something so much?"

Dr. Goodsell nodded. "It's possible," she said. "They're not so different from us, really."

Mrs. Monroe looked at Jasper. He met her eyes, steady

on. Then she stood up and walked over beside J.D. "Joy?" she asked. "Would it help at all?"

It took her a minute to answer. I saw her wipe her nose again. But finally she managed to nod. "Yes," she said, so low I almost didn't hear her. And then, even lower, "Please."

Mama gave me another look. We shouldn'ta been staring. It wasn't good manners, I know. But right before I dropped my eyes, I saw Mrs. Monroe put her hand on J.D.'s shoulder. And for once, for just this once, she didn't pull away.

CHAPTER thirty-seven

We didn't take the Empress home that same night. Dr. Goodsell didn't think she could stand another trip so soon. She said she could maybe bend the rules a little bit and keep her just a few more days, till she wasn't feeling so parched out and all.

It was pretty hard leaving her there, still hooked up to them tubes and everything. But the doctor promised to take care of her, and we knew she would. So we just looked in on her for a minute, and petted her good-night, and she blinked them big eyes once and went right back to sleep. And then we all piled in Mrs. Monroe's car, and Jasper drove us home.

The first stars were just coming out when we pulled in our driveway.

Mama and Daddy didn't lecture us too much that night, which I thought was real nice, considering how bad we'd scared 'em. They just fed us some macaroni and cheese and put us to bed and said we'd talk about it in the morning. Which we did, of course. Lord, did we.

Turned out they'd started looking for us less'n a half hour after we climbed on that first bus, soon as Mrs. Monroe noticed that J.D. had gone missing at the mansion.

"So she called over here to see if y'all knew where she was, and then I called over't the Smiths to see could I catch you before you left for the zoo, and naturally Mrs. Smith answered the phone and didn't know what in the heck I was talking about."

"I'm sorry, Daddy. I really am. I swear I'll never tell another lie as long as I live. The bus was leaving—it was all I could think of right then."

Daddy raised his eyebrows. "You might've tried the truth. I could've been there in five minutes. We'da figured some way to help that little girl."

He was right, of course. Simplest thing in the world. I could see it clear as daylight now. Funny how at the time it was happening, it never even crossed my mind.

I wondered would it have turned out the same if I'd thought of that one little thing.

"Well, thank God you mentioned the zoo, at least," said Mama. "Otherwise we wouldn't have had any idea. But by the time Joy's mother called Mrs. Monroe from Houston, we were able to put two and two together."

My mouth dropped open. "J.D.'s mother called Mrs. Monroe? But I thought they couldn't stand one another!"

"Well, they've both had a real hard time, but it sounds like they're trying to work everything out for Joy's sake. Clarice was just frantic when y'all showed up over there and then left so quick. She said one of y'all had on a big coat and was hiding something under it. So then we called the zoo and asked 'em to keep an eye out for three kids and a monkey, and that nice security guard had seen you walking in not twenty minutes before."

Well, I'll be dogged. We'd left a trail a mile wide, hadn't we? Not to mention me flat out telling 'em where to look. I guess I can count out that career in espionage.

So anyhow we talked it all out, and once they understood the whole thing, they were a lot nicer about it than I ever expected. They even looked at each other funny when I got to the part about the ninety bucks, like they kind of felt bad for me. Course it didn't keep me from getting grounded for a while, but I guess they figured losing my trip to Phoenix ought to be counted in, too. So when Mrs. Monroe called the next week and asked if me and Mary Al would like to drive over with her and Jasper and J.D. to pick up the Empress, they actually said yes.

And you talk about a great day. That little furball was feeling so much better'n the last time we seen her we couldn't even hardly believe it. She seemed real glad to see us, too—climbing all over us and messing with our hair and chittering away in our ears. It was enough to make you smile for a month.

"Maybe I could spend that money I been saving and

buy her a husband monkey," Mary Al said on the way home. "And he can be the Emperor of Elsewhere, and they can have little monkey babies, and they'll all live happily ever after."

But Mrs. M said she believed we'd just take it one step at a time for now. . . .

Meanwhile, the Empress ain't a bit lonesome, with us taking her to the island every day. It's October now, and she's back to her old self again. It'd do your heart good to see her swinging through the branches and eating frogs and throwing nuts at old Thursday. I swear I believe she missed the maniac a little. She even chases *him* every now and then, just for a change of pace.

Course we still got a good bit of work to do. I was over there after school just today with J.D. and Mary Al, trying to figure out how to rig the window some way that's squirrel-proof and monkey-friendly, but I ain't quite got it yet. Daddy says once I settle on my plan and know what parts I need, I can probably use his employee's discount over at Wal-Mart. I might just end up inventing something so good, I'll get me one of them patents and make a million bucks. Or at least enough to go see the Grand Canyon one of these days.

"Maybe we'll go together," J.D. said. "I'd kind of like to see it again."

"Maybe so," I said. "I guess you can't really see it too many times."

She shook her head. "Well, depends on who you are.

When we went, my folks and I were standing on the rim looking at it, really enjoying the view and everything, and after we were there awhile, this guy came and stood right by us with his kid—looked like he was twelve or thirteen. So they stared out there for about two minutes, and then the kid said, "Okay, what's next?" And his dad got all upset—he kept saying, "What's *next*? What do you mean, what's next? This is the Grand Canyon—what we drove two thousand miles to see. There *is* no next, Cleon—this is it."

Well, we laughed about that, but then I started thinking—you know, I don't really blame old Cleon. I kind of like wondering what's next myself. So maybe it's better that I ain't seen it yet. I mean, I got my whole life, right? And something that big—well, I don't mind having it ahead of me, that's all.

Anyhow, things are going just fine, and I got no complaints worth mentioning. It's cooled off quite a bit, which has everybody cheered up considerable. Even Mrs. Monroe—funny thing I noticed, when we stopped in the music room today? Now that it's not so hot outside, it ain't such an icebox in there. She had all the windows open and the breeze blowing and the sun pouring in, and when I shook her hand it was warm as anybody's. There was music playing, too—just something on an old record player, but it sounded awful nice. "The Beautiful Isle of Somewhere" the man was singing, which I thought was a real strange coincidence. Mrs. Monroe was looking out at *our* island at the time and talking about how maybe she'd better build that bridge, after all, just to be on the safe side. J.D. seemed real pleased about that, but there ain't any rush, now that we got our boat back. We have new oars, and plenty of life jackets, and Jasper staring at us every time we go across, anyhow. . . .

Let's see now—there's just a couple more things you ought to know, and that should pretty much do it. Did I tell you J.D.'s going to my school? Course it was kind of shaky at the start. In the first week alone she got sent home three times—once for cussing and twice for biting Conrad Smith. But then I ain't one to hold a little thing like that against her. And she seems to be settling down pretty well now. She says her mom's doing better, too. They might even look for a place over here, once she gets back on her feet a bit more, so J.D. can still see the Empress and not have to change schools again.

I think it was that psychologist lady who suggested it. J.D. don't call her old Nosy Rosy now. We were talking about her just today in the tree house—turns out she was the one who told Mrs. Monroe back in June that J.D. ought to have some company her age. Which was why them screechified girls that started the whole mess got invited over in the first place.

"So in other words, if we traveled back in time and killed the dinosaur that ought to have been supper for Dr. Rosenberg's great-great-grandmother, we wouldn't even be having this conversation?"

J.D. grinned and punched me on the arm. "You never did finish reading that book, did you, James Henry?"

Well, no. I didn't. I never got past the first paragraph. And I still don't know what *recondite* means, but I ain't gonna sweat it. I figure it happened the way it happened, that's all, and on a day like today I'm real glad it did— with the sun shining and the sweet gums redding up and all the trees purring and the birds singing their hearts out and Mary Al down there playing hide-and-seek with the Empress and old crazy Thursday, and me and my friend J.D. setting up here in our tree house.

If that ain't happily ever after, it'll sure do for now.

Special thanks and love to my husband,
Kevin Cooney;

to our sons,
Michael Christopher, Brian David,
and Errol Andrew;

and to my editor and friend,
Richard Jackson.

Many thanks also to
Sister Hilary, Sister Fatima, and all the
Sisters of Charity at St. Elizabeth's Hospital,
formerly the estate of Mr. and Mrs. John Henry
Phelan;

to David Cooney; Bill Greene;
Clare Fields Flood; and Jennifer Fields Hawkins
(the original Mrs. Million Dillion);

and especially to
my unforgettable Aunt Pat,
Patricia Phelan Milam;

and to all my Phelan cousins—
Patsy, Johnny, Frankie, David, Mary Ann, and
Jimmy—*who once had a monkey named Nicky.*

Theresa Nelson is the author of five other novels, four of which were cited as *School Library Journal* Best Books of the Year: *The 25¢ Miracle*; *And One for All*; *The Beggars' Ride*; and *Earthshine*, a 1995 *Boston Globe/Horn Book* Honor Book and an ALA Best Book for Young Adults. She lives in Sherman Oaks, California, and is married to actor Kevin Cooney. They are the parents of three grown sons.